THE
SHORT STORIES
OF
RON IDDON

THE
QUEENSLAND
COLLECTION

Published by Leopardwood Productions, P. O. Box 4818, Toowoomba East, Queensland, 4350, Australia.

Iddon, Ron 1940—

The Short Stories of Ron Iddon---The Queensland Collection

ISBN 978-0-646-57585-8

Lives, past and present, in rural Queensland

Book design by Steven Wilson of Cranbrook Press, Toowoomba, Queensland, Australia

Virtual Author's Assistant Lyn Prowse-Bishop, Executive Stress Office Support, Warwick, Queensland, Australia

Type-set in Trajan Pro and Palatino, 9 – 22 pt

Printed and bound by Lulu.com

THE STORIES

A SHORT NOTE TO THE READER

Welcome

Australia's giant northern state of Queensland has provided a home for me for over twenty years---both roomy and rewarding--- so I thought it time to pay something back.

As in my earlier book, "The Murray River Collection", the settings for these stories are rural---but I think the themes are universal. Also as in that previous book, many of the stories are written in the first person, and as a different character each time; in one, "A Colourful Life", I am a Silky Oak kitchen dresser.

A---kindly---critic has written that I am at times more of a 'chronicler' than 'creative storyteller'; "Pearl" and "Her Hair" will perhaps re-inforce that view. I *can* say that both of those stories are in fact from my imagination---but what both of them do attest to is a bias towards choosing women as my subjects. Until recently it has definitely been I believe a man's world; women have had to be especially clever and resourceful to achieve and even survive in it, and that makes them especially interesting to me.

***

Friends have told me they find my stories easy to read. Writers who harbour literary pretensions could be disturbed by such comments---might find them almost derogatory---could even let themselves become depressed by them---but I say yes!

Ron Iddon
June 2012

ACKNOWLEDGEMENTS

To my editor, Letitia Gregory of Melbourne, whose robust and reasoned criticisms have only ever spurred me on.

And to all those friends---and members of my family---who have encouraged me.

ONE

HER ANSWER

After ten years with the truck Wal still didn't know which trip he liked best, this one---the Monday one down to the coast---or the Thursday one inland. The coast one was much shorter, but then there was that long haul back up in the afternoon with the sun in his eyes. There were no hills on the western run, and he loved pushing the Commer to forty miles an hour across the plains, but it was twice as far, and with very little bitumen. With the horses it had definitely been the coast run because it had taken only two days as against four---but with the truck he didn't really know.

He turned into the main street now and pulled up at the café. He could see the little box on the step and he knew that inside there'd be the long list rolled up in an elastic band. It had surprised him at first, what they went through in a week; no wonder people said it was a good business.

No passenger this time. Pity---he always liked it when Sophia came with him for the day to visit relatives. She was a lovely girl; Belle liked to kid him about her, but she liked her too.

As he got back up behind the wheel he turned off the lights; didn't really need them by September. He drove off again past the hotel and the houses, quietly so as not to wake people. Peg Shields was up though, watering her trees at the front. He gave her a wave.

***

"Sophia, you have to talk to us." Outside on the footpath some dry leaves swirled, and the girl opened one of the doors and went out to sweep. She liked this time of year; her town friends complained about the Dry but the cattle people who came in just seemed to accept it.

Her mother had followed. "People will be here soon. We have to talk." But there would be no-one for half an hour and then only old Peg for her Monday treat---and she was almost deaf. Sophia began to sweep, her long brown hair swinging. The early sun touched her arms and legs, turning them golden.

"You can't just keep thinking of yourself. What about the Gambinis? They've spent a lot of money." The young woman stopped sweeping; the older woman glanced back into the café.

"Mama....," but now her father was there. "Your mother's right. It's time you thought about other people." And her friend Lizzie Collins was always telling her she should start thinking about herself.

"Papa, are you asking me to be considerate to Mick Gambini?"

"Yes." Something in her tone; he began to rub at the already shining brass door handle.

"Mick Gambini has brought that boy out here as slave labour and if I married him he would get two slaves."

"Sophia!"

"Well it's true, Mama. Ask Paulo. Ask Mrs Gambini."

"They work together. We all do. The Gambinis are a very happy family."

She finished sweeping and walked up the steps, put the broom on its stand and went behind the counter. Her parents came and stood on the other side and seemed to be waiting for her to speak. "He opens their money boxes."

"Who says?"

"Teresa."

"Girls shouldn't have money."

"The boys' too. Paulo's eighteen!"

The doorbell jangled, the three looked over and Peg Shields was there.

***

I seem to have caught them on the hop, she thought. She looked across at the grandfather clock that stood in one corner and saw that she was a little early but the trio had already gone straight to work, setting a table and making the cocoa and the cinnamon toast. She always liked to watch them---they worked so well together.

Was it her imagination or was there a special air? Had she interrupted something? The girl's movements were particularly quick, and there was high colour in her face. Just blooming that girl.

They were saying things---more than usual---but she could scarcely hear speech these days. Now she was given extra toast, and the cocoa was creamier. Yes---something was on.

***

Their tasks completed the three stood together again near the counter. The man changed the tone of his voice. "Sophia, this Gambini boy will be right for you. He will make a good husband. Tell her what Maria said."

"She said her sister says he's her best boy. No trouble. Always does what he's told." A laugh burst from the girl, then she looked down at the floor; after a long pause she took a deep breath. "I am not marrying someone I don't know."

"You'll have lots of time to get to know each other."

"You mean, after the wedding? Like you and Papa?"

"Yes, like me and your father. It's a good way."

Sophia looked at her mother but the older woman looked away. Her father hit the counter with his hand. "You will marry this boy we have chosen for you!" As he walked out to the kitchen she touched her mother's hand.

***

Three days later and Peg Shields, barefoot and still in her nightdress, is standing on the verandah looking through the half closed wooden louvres. It is cool, and she wraps her bare arms around herself, but remains where she is. Always her favourite time of the day, even when she'd had children to feed and a man to get off to work.

There is a movement down on the lawn near the bougainvillea; Red has walked around from the back and is looking up at her. How did he know I was standing here? Silly question---old dogs know everything.

Now he's turning and walking up the driveway and out the gate. He stands still, looking along towards the shops, and then begins wagging his tail.

She moves closer to the louvres in time to see the girl reach the dog. She has a bag, and puts it down and bends to pat Red. Now both are looking up the street, and after a moment Peg too hears the truck; oh, she's going down with Wal---must be going to stay a while this time. The kettle whistles and she goes through to the kitchen.

She has half finished a cup before she remembers it's a Thursday.

TWO

A COLOURFUL LIFE

I was made by a Fred Withers in 1907. Fred was one of our town's best furniture craftsmen and was commissioned by Gordon Bartlam and Sons Emporium to make a number of kitchen dressers for sale in their shop. They were to be of pine, New Zealand Kauri I think, considered at that time, would you believe, to be superior to our beautiful Queensland timbers.

Fred did not have quite enough pine for all six so for me he used some nice Silky Oak that he had been saving. As you know, it is a timber that has very distinctive grains, and mine are unusually well developed. Fred went to a lot of trouble with my grains to produce pleasing patterns but Mr Bartlam, amazingly, was not happy, and only agreed to take me at a lower price. I was put on the showroom floor at a lower price too and was in fact the first of the consignment sold---possibly because I was the cheapest---but I'd like to think it was also because I was much more eyecatching than the others. I know that Ern Fogarty did think I was better *value*. "That one's solid---the kids won't wreak it."

The Fogartys were just moving into their new home, one with much more room for their five children. It was actually an old house, what they call nowadays a 'colonial', a typical large tropical house, on high stumps with a steep roof and a bull nose verandah on all sides; it had tall French windows leading from most rooms onto that verandah. Lots of iron lace work.

I was put in the kitchen of course---in a spot that I was to occupy uninterruptedly for the next seventy years. I thought it was a nice room, with high ceilings, two tall windows, a big slow combustion stove and built-in cupboards along one side from floor to ceiling. The food safes and later the ice chests were kept underneath the house.

***

As kitchen dressers go I am big, over eight feet long and seven feet high; what's that today---two and a half metres by two. That was possibly another reason the Fogartys picked me---they had a big family and a big house.

It occurs to me that you may not know what old Australian kitchen dressers looked like so I shall describe myself. I have a series of shelves, open, with solid timber sides, and a pair of cupboards beneath---one cupboard really, but with two doors. You will frequently see pieces like me in antique shops---of pine usually, and often stripped down to the bare timber, and sometimes waxed. They dress us up for sale with rows of plates along the shelves, the plates kept upright by being leaned behind thin wooden strips which are secured along the upper surface of each shelf; if you did not know the strips were there you probably would not notice them.

We also have hooks screwed in along the front edges of the shelves and the vertical sides, on which cups are hung. Over time these tend to rust or work loose, and get lost; often people did not bother to replace them. Mine were originally made of black steel, but now I have brass ones. I have four shelves, one more than the average--- but I *am* bigger than the average.

My sides are called *waterfalls,* and I shall try to describe these. If you were to look at me from the side, and let your eye run down from the very top, where I am quite narrow, you would see that I widen a little in a curve at a certain point, and continue on down at that greater width---as a waterfall does after it has hit a ledge. I have *two* such 'events' down my side and these I believe make me look less utilitarian; people sometimes describe me as *Victorian*---though I was built in the Edwardian era---and I think it is partly because of my 'waterfalls'.

My cupboards are deep, and can hold a lot. There are fly screens at the sides, so that fresh food can be stored in here. Originally mine were made of perforated zinc sheeting, and you still see some of this around. My sheeting had crumbled by the late 1940's and Ern Fogarty replaced it with modern fly wire. He did a neat job but it looked out of place for a long time---too shiny; over time it darkened though and blended in again.

When I was introduced into the house in 1907 the kitchen had just been painted---duck egg blue. Do you know that colour? It's a cool dark blue, with a touch of green. I thought my golden grains looked good against it but after a few weeks Mavis Fogarty told her husband that she wanted him to *paint me the same colour;* she felt I "stood out" too much. "And it's so big!"

Ern protested, saying it would be a pity to hide my grain and patterns, but she was insistent and duck egg blue I became---just the first of several colour changes I would have to endure during my life. At least Ern did a very thorough job of it, a fact to which future owners who tried to remove his results could attest.

***

Mavis and Ern Fogarty eventually had seven children. The littlees liked to play games in my cupboards but their feet played hell with that thin zinc sheeting. The children used my cupboard tops too; the door from the verandah was just to my right, and it was always used by the kids when they came home from school. Kids always seem to visit kitchens first don't they; Mum's there---or was in those days---and of course they're always hungry.

My nice big flat cupboard top must have seemed the most natural place on which to dump school bags and books and whatever was in their pockets---sometimes even live things, like lizards and baby birds.

Mavis grumbled at first about this annexation of her 'counter' but she gave up after a while; she never tried to keep anything of her own there, certainly nothing 'good'. She did forbid her children the use of the shelves above, and here she displayed her nice blue and white plates. These were rarely used; the everyday stuff was kept in tall built-ins along one of the walls.

Occupying most of the floor area of the kitchen was a long wide pine table, unpainted and kept clean by frequent scrubbing. You could seat at least sixteen people around it, and sometimes there *were* that many---visiting uncles and aunts and cousins, or just friends of the children who happened to be in the house at meal times.

That table was the hub of the family's life, at mealtimes of course (there was no separate dining room, or if there were it was never used as such), and for making bread and jam, and for every kind of food preparation---and for dress-making, opening the mail, patching up minor wounds, doing homework, family conferences--- everything.

***

It was a noisy household, with kids of all ages competing to be heard, but I think all round it was a happy one. Any grievances were short lived. Mavis and Ern were very warm with each other: lots of hugs and kisses.

***

Mavis Fogarty was a hard working woman; all mothers worked hard in those days, making meals, sewing and darning, cleaning, washing---which took a whole day in that household---and ironing, which was often done at night, and once again on that big table.

Mrs. McCready, a widow, used to come in and help Mavis with mending and sewing, and sometimes the ironing, and you never heard more chatter and laughter. Mrs McCready had high little cheeks that would turn crimson when she laughed and in that kitchen they were *always* crimson. I think Mavis Fogarty had the happiest hours of her week then---and I wouldn't say all that much work was actually done.

***

The saddest day I recall was when we got the news that the eldest boy William had been killed, on the Western Front; he was only twenty. Mavis must have opened the telegram at the front door and she came into the kitchen calling "oh Ernie, Ernie......" The two of them sat at the table for over an hour, he with his arm over her shoulder.

Right through the afternoon he came in and out but she didn't move, not even when the children came home from school. About dark Ern led Mavis away, and the eldest girls got dinner ready.

***

By 1935 all the children had left and the couple were living on their own in that big house. Ern died in 1951 but Mavis continued on there by herself. She had lots of visits from friends and family though---and she still made scones and cakes---on that table--- and used the old fuel stove.

When she died in 1957 her family decided to sell the house, her children all having their own houses by then. No-one wanted any of the larger pieces of furniture from the house---not even me! They left it up to the real estate agent; if the eventual buyers of the house liked any pieces they could have them for whatever the agent thought reasonable. The rest could be given away.

***

Helen Morrison took a long while to make up her mind about me. She stood in front, frowning, then walked back and forwards, looking at me from different angles---went to another room and then came back again. Finally she said to her husband "I think we'll keep this. Don't like the colour but the piece is really rather nice." *Rather nice!*

The kitchen was painted white and Jack Morrison had to paint me white too. Laminex was all the go then and the old pine table had to go, along with the plain wooden chairs.

The laminex on the new table was a sort of strawberry and white; the new chairs were chromed and padded. It was a smallish table, only about five feet long, and I thought it looked far too small for the room. I hoped that the big old table was cherished by whoever bought it ---such a lot of living around that old thing. I wonder where it is now?

Helen and Jack had two teenaged children, a boy and a girl, but there were not to be many family gatherings around the laminex. Jack was a car salesman and was gone nearly all day every day, often on weekends too. Helen Morrison did prepare substantial evening meals but even the children seemed to have things to do that kept them away then---sport or ballet or other things. It was only perhaps once a week that all four sat down together for an evening meal.

Helen did not work---for wages---but did she keep a busy schedule! She must have been on just about every committee our town had---Rotary Ladies, the Debutante Ball, the Jerusalem Home for the Aged---everything. Sometimes her committee would meet in her house and she would prepare for this with great vigour, dusting and cleaning, and making sandwiches and cooking slices; she did everything thoroughly. She did herself up thoroughly too; she always looked immaculate.

It was such a difference to the lives of my previous owners---in several ways; Jack and Helen had many arguments. There were bitter words from her, about being neglected.

A Les Jackson came onto the scene; he worked at the same car place as Jack. When he called in with Jack he would flirt with Helen, and when Les began to call on his own what happened went a long way past flirting. I don't want to seem crude, but I don't know what use that old pine table might have been put to if it had still been there!

Nevertheless Helen and Jack Morrison did stay together. Their Sharon went to stay with her aunt in Brisbane to do a secretarial course and I did not see her again. She was a lively independent sort of girl and I think would have done well in anything she tackled. Jeremy got an apprenticeship and after a year moved out to live with two other apprentices in their own flat here in town. He would drop in now and then, sometimes with one of his mates. He has his own electrician's business here now.

In 1977 Helen and Jack Morrison decided to move to the coast. They advertised 'a houseful of furniture' in the local paper---they were taking none of us with them---and there were streams of lookers. I was bought by the Hintons.

***

The Hinton home had one long verandah that had been enclosed and that now served as bedroom for their three little girls; I was to become their all-purpose storage space. Dolls and bears and other toys were crammed into my cupboards, and books and crayons and what-have-you were piled on the tops. The girls could use the lowest of my shelves, but Penny Hinton did not allow them to use the higher ones because they would need to climb up and could pull me over onto them. I have not mentioned that my top is not attached to my base, but simply rests on it. It is well balanced though.

The girls were delightful---but what an undignified life I now led. Once again I had children hiding and wrestling in my cupboards, so that once again I lost both of my end screens. Robert Hinton took them out completely and boarded me up. And the girls were allowed to paint me, or more accurately paint *on* me, and soon big patches of orange and green and yellow had been added to the white. All very bright---nothing pastel or subtle. And underneath I was Silky Oak!

The eldest girl was given her own bedroom when she was eight or so and the same with the next until Jessica eventually had the whole verandah to herself. In 1990 when she was about sixteen she decided she wanted to repaint the whole room---pink---and she wanted different furniture; I was too *gross*.

The Hintons put a 'For Sale' ad in the local paper and I was bought for a pittance---remember my colours---by a schoolteacher who had just been transferred here and was furnishing a house with several other teachers. In that move my top and my base were transported separately and I was not put back together but placed side by side against one wall of my new owner's bedroom. Someone had told Jennifer that I *could* be Silky Oak and she informed her housemates she had had a Silky Oak dressing table when she was a child which she loved; "I'm going to restore this," she declared.

Music to my ears---but she hadn't counted on the thoroughness of some of my previous decorators. She started on my cupboards; the paint that the Hinton girls had put on came off easily enough but Jack Morrison's white proved a tougher proposition. She decided to concentrate on just one small patch of it. "I must see the original timber," she told anyone who came to inspect progress, but of course what she did see next was Ern Fogarty's duck egg blue. This proved to have all the attributes of armour plating and after repeated applications of stripper and much scraping she gave up. Jennifer never did get to see even one square inch of the original me.

My shelves and my now somewhat disfigured cupboard base stood side by side in her bedroom until one of the other teachers in the house got a promotion to a school in a village about an hour inland from our town and 'borrowed' my top as a bookcase. After she had settled in there she took it into her head to paint me: *crimson*.

From1993 onward then I lived two entirely separate lives, one as an open bright red bookcase in a hinterland village with Elaine and one in town here with Jennifer as a sturdy but somewhat tortured looking two door cupboard.

It got worse in 1995. Jennifer was herself promoted to a big school two hundred miles further up the coast and gave me---the bottom half of me---to the handyman father of one of her students, who had mentioned that he wanted a cupboard for his garage. It did not matter to him that my paintwork had been abused; hardly anyone was going to see me anyhow. I was put against one wall and soon filled with tins of paint and grease and a jumble of tools, and anything and everything was dumped on top. I got very dirty; I had sunk very low.

***

In 1996 Elaine moved from her village back into town---a promotion for her---and she brought the crimson bookcase part of me back with her. She gave me to Tricia, a younger teacher who had just moved here, but within a year she too was given a promotion to another town and I found myself at Lifeline's Opportunity Shop.

Old Mrs.Chisholm who ran the shop knew quite a lot about old furniture and recognised my shelves for what they were. I heard her say to another of the women "you know that's a real tragedy. That's the top of one of those old kitchen dressers. It's heavy too---could even be Silky Oak." She put me up on a table in a corner of the shop and within a few days Prue Harper bought me.

This was in 1998 and Prue would have been about thirty five then. She had grown up here, gone to Uni in Brisbane and studied Law and then married Ben her childhood sweetheart, who had stayed and worked on his father's fruit farm, which is just on the edge of town. He had done a distance degree in agricultural business as well. He and Prue set up house in the town so that she could practise as a solicitor; they had had three children.

Prue, who had some experience at restoring, started on my shelves. Off came the crimson then the white and finally---she was more determined than my previous owner---the first of of Ern Fogarty's duck egg blue. She knew now that she had Silky Oak, and she set herself the goal of finding my base. She began to answer any sale ad that mentioned old Australian furniture, and to attend all the clearing sales in our district.

***

Last year two big things happened---big for me. The Harpers had been keeping their eyes out for a bigger house and my old one came on the market. Prue, who had always admired it, looked at it as soon as she read about it and dragged Ben there that night. Ben asked a builder friend to check it out the next morning; on his advice they made an offer straight away and the offer was accepted.

When they made the move they stored the bookshelf part of me in the big shed in the backyard. Then Ben happened to go into a friend's garage and notice a sturdy cupboard against a wall. With the owner's permission he measured the height and width and gave the figures to his wife. Prue knew her search was over as soon as she entered the garage. The man said she could have me for a six pack; she gave him a whole carton.

She put both parts of me side by side in the shed and told her husband she would do all the restoring herself. That took her many, many weeks; getting the last of the old blue out of the vertical joins in my back was what took the most effort. When she had finally achieved that she gave me a thorough turps wash.

I was now naked looking and quite characterless, pale and seemingly without any grain at all, like a piece of anonymous new plantation timber that one might see in a hardware store. For a few weeks Prue left me like that---she was going through a very busy time at work I think---or perhaps she just wanted a break from me---and then one evening she came into the garage and began to apply a light shellac. "I just want to seal the timber," she told her husband. "I don't want a high shine."

I remember how happy she became as she worked, as I turned an orange gold before her eyes, and all my grain and patterns emerged. I think in her eyes I would have *glowed*. (Please forgive the effusiveness, but---it *had* been a hundred years).

She was so thrilled she called Ben and even the children to come and see. Over the next two weeks, at night, Prue worked on all my surfaces. When she was satisfied, she had me carried back up to the kitchen, and I was put in the same position that had been mine for so long all those years ago.

***

One of Prue's friends, when she was brought in to see me, suggested I be given *several* coats of shellac, but Prue said that that would darken me, and also make me shiny, and that was not what she wanted. "I want to *see* that timber. I want to *feel* it." Didn't I love to hear those words.

***

And so here I am today, just where I want to be and looking just as I should. I am much admired by visitors---but I think my restorer and owner actually *loves* me. She will frequently stand in front of me, cup of tea or coffee in hand, just gazing. Sometimes she will move closer and run a hand along a shelf, and down my side. *My waterfall side.*

THREE

LIZ AND ME

It was a hot afternoon on "Bull Run" and I'd come up from the cattle yards to have a drink and a rest. Liz was ironing some of the kids' clothes in the lounge room and I lay down on the floorboards nearby. She was barefooted, and whenever an ankle came within reach I massaged it, something she loved.

She stopped ironing. "When did you first realise you fancied me?"

"*Fancied* you?"

"You know, what---attracted you?"

My hand crept out but ankles stayed out of reach. "Everything."

She thumped one foot on the boards. " Hugh!"

"Do you mean---*the* moment?"

"Yes."

***

I certainly was not immediately attracted to Liz. On my early visits to Bull Run she had registered with me as just a tomboy, a dusty worker hardly distinguishable from her father's stockmen. Added to that she was ten centimetres taller than yours truly, and I had never been attracted to tall girls.

I was twenty-three years of age and had just come up from the south. Two years before this I had graduated from Melbourne University, in Agricultural Economics, and had taken a job with one of the big pastoral agencies in that state. I was happy enough in my work, giving advice to agency clients, but then I read an advertisement by a group of Central Queensland graziers; they wanted someone to help them get better returns from their properties.

I liked the thought of it---big places and big operations; it would be an adventure---*and* a job I thought I could handle. As it turned out this whiz kid was to spend two years *taking in* more knowledge than he imparted---something about which his employers proved to be very forbearing.

Their properties were in the district that surrounded a town called Redspear. I set up house in the town itself but spent most of my time out on the places themselves, and particularly at Bull Run. This large station, a hundred kilometres north of the town, was owned by the chairman of the group, Jack Dunn. His dining room, with its enormous cedar table, became my second office; many of the group's meetings took place around that table.

***

Jack was a widower, his wife having been killed in a driving accident many years before. He ran the property now with Liz, his only child, and she always sat in on any of the group's meetings.

Liz didn't say much at these times, perhaps just asking a question or two, and I have to say she did not at first make much of an impression on me. I guess I was full of the challenge of the new job. Probably full of myself too. Initially I thought she was only eighteen or nineteen, when she was actually twenty-two.

Her face would eventually become the dearest and most beautiful thing in the world to me, but even after several months I would have been unable to describe the colour of her eyes---even what her face *actually looked like*. She and I would sit across from each other at that table, yet had I ever really looked at those calm features, and into those hazel pools?

Later I would realise that Liz did not often look anyone full in the face, and when I mentioned this she said it was because she felt that when she did so it only reminded people of her height. "I was always tall---even at school. I was taller than all the boys."

Apparently it had become a habit, this looking off to one side during a conversation, and even with people taller than herself. After we talked about it though she dropped the habit, and almost overnight.

***

If our meetings or my work went on late into the night I would sleep at the Run, and if I had no appointments the next day I would help out with whatever was happening on the station. It was good when the Dunns had cattle in the yards, and I could help them with drafting or dipping or whatever, or when a big mob had to be mustered. If I may say so myself, I was able to make myself pretty useful, courtesy of skills I'd learned as a boy.

I began to be very impressed with Liz's abilities. She was a bold rider; she could estimate accurately the weight of a bullock and recite the pedigree of a bull. She could spot a conformation fault in an animal before anyone else.

I began to *like* her too---and she seemed to like me. She made this southern 'know-all' feel welcome.

***

At that time there were five stockmen employed on Bull Run plus a cook/housekeeper and her husband, the gardener/handyman. The staff ate in a room attached to the kitchen, which was separated from the homestead by a covered walkway. The owners and any guests were supposed to eat in the house itself, in that big dining room, but most of the time there were only Jack and Elizabeth there and they preferred to eat out with the staff.

Jack did not take the seat at the head of the table, and in fact he avoided it. He had initiated the custom of putting the newest stockman in it. Early in his occupancy of the chair, and when Jack thought he was ready, the newcomer was asked to tell everyone about his earlier life. This created some fun and at times perhaps some embarrassment for the new chum but it certainly broke the ice. Jack waited only two nights before he asked me to tell my story.

The men, and Deb the cook, all called Jack 'Mister' but that was the limit of any formality. Jack seemed to relish dinner times, and as soon as talk about local affairs flagged would bring up topics of national and international news. He challenged anyone who made a sweeping statement; it did not take a newcomer long to realise that a loose opinion would be pounced upon---but it all made for a lively time.

I was spending mealtimes at tables in homesteads all through the district at that time but none were more interesting or stimulating than those in the 'outside' room at Bull Run.

***

One afternoon, about nine months after I had taken up the job, I was going over some cash flow sheets on the dining room table when Jack called me out onto the back verandah. Across the flat below the homestead a single rider was leading a mob of perhaps three hundred prime bullocks. They were walking slowly, and the late sun was setting their shiny red coats afire. A blue cattle dog was bringing up the rear. The rider, on a white horse, was Liz.

"Nice sight," said Jack, somewhere between a statement and a question. I nodded, but I was looking only at Liz---so competent and so calm; something went click inside me.

***

"That!? Me on a horse!?"

"It was a very nice horse---Dillon I think."

"Duke."

"And they were beautiful Santas."

" Droughties."

"See?" I stretched out my arm. "I wasn't really looking at them."

Liz snorted and resumed ironing, but after a while began humming one of the old hymns she liked. An ankle came within reach, and stayed.

***

At breakfast the next morning Liz asked "well, don't you want to know?"

"Okay---when?"

Silence. I raised my eyebrows and she blushed.

"C'mon...."

"Alright." She gathered herself. "That night you were sitting at the head of the table and we asked you about your home down south."

"Why? What did I say?"

"You made it sound so nice. All your brothers. Your Mum and Dad. A real family."

"It wasn't always nice."

"I suppose. But it seemed nice to me. Anyhow, it made *you* nice." I got a kiss.

***

We lived in a town in the west of Victoria and my father was a senior employee of a big livestock agency. There was a takeover by another company and the new owners offered Dad the local managership. It would have meant a big increase in salary but he decided instead to start his own agency. *Their* agency: it would have been very much a joint decision between Mother and Dad.

We four boys had always been involved in Dad's work, even when we were little, helping him load and unload sheep and cattle at the saleyards, and penning up and keeping tallies, and when the family struck out on its own we all became even busier, but we were older and I suppose more useful by then.

My own children would eventually help out on Bull Run in the same way, but more willingly I think. I and my brothers were always handling someone else's livestock but on the Run these were their own horses they saddled and their own cattle they rounded up and I'm sure that made a difference. I remember being not at all keen to get up at six on a Victorian winter's morning to go to the local saleyards and unload someone's fat lambs, but at the Run, if we had an early muster, there would be our bunch out on the verandah at dawn, tucking shirts into jeans and pulling on their elastic sided boots. Stumbling and still half asleep. Liz and I would stand at the kitchen door and watch the performance.

***

Dad used to give each of us a lot of responsibility yet I don't remember getting many *instructions* from him. And not much 'fathering'---moral guidance, that kind of thing. I think that when one is the youngest of four boys that sort of thing probably gets done quite capably by one's brothers.

Mother was different. She was a stickler for 'manners', and we were frequently given instructions in that department. Katherine's father had been a bank manager, and at that time---in that town---his family would have been considered 'society'. Katherine went to boarding school, and often stayed during holidays with school friends on their properties, in homesteads that were and are some of the grandest in the country.

It seemed to us boys that our speech and our manners were always being corrected by her---but perhaps our mixing with the stockmen at the saleyards made that necessary. We were always being told that something was "not a suitable expression." When I think back, Mother must have heard an awful lot that was 'unsuitable', but I don't seem to remember her becoming either shocked or angry. She always spoke politely to us, and in that special Western districts accent which is so distinct and familiar that I can still pick it today. Dad didn't speak with the accent, which is strange because he mixed a lot with people who did; perhaps the sons of grocers just did not speak that way.

Would you believe Mother used to leave *calling cards,* and we had a little silver dish on a table in the front hall for other people's cards (not that many left them). She also preserved the custom of not answering the front door herself; only if there were absolutely no other people in the house at all would Mother go to the door. She might not have been 'at home' you see.

When she did meet people however she always asked after their families. She was *so* interested that they eventually told her about their more distant relatives as well, uncles and cousins and the like, and about anything and everything that was happening in their part of the country, *and she seemed to remember it all.* In later years district writers and historians were always phoning or visiting her; if she did not know something about some person or event she was usually able to refer them to someone who did.

Later I urged her to put her recollections on paper or at least on tape, but it did not happen. I should have gone down and seen to it myself; when she died the Western Districts of Victoria lost an encyclopaedia.

Anyhow, as I was saying, there was this level of formality in our upbringing. We used to whinge about the lessons in manners, but of course bits stuck. Later I realised they actually had a practical value. Apart from anything else they do allow one to screen or deter without causing embarrassment. As I remember Mother once saying, "you can laugh about dance cards but I was able to shake off more than one unsuitable beau with a 'full' card."

***

We had finished breakfast and there were many things to do, for both of us, but we were dawdling. I caught Liz looking at me.

"What?"

That sweet smile. "Your mother."

"Yes?"

"She asked me once how you courted me."

I laughed: she did too.

***

We'd mustered a mob of heifers and were poking home in the late afternoon on a couple of tired horses. I had closed the last gate but hadn't yet remounted. We were talking, and I was leaning against her horse's neck. Liz's hand was resting on its wither right beside my face and I kissed it. She leaned down and kissed me on the lips. That was it really----engaged.

FOUR

THE BEGUMS OF NAMBOUR

"Harriet rang a little while ago." I had given my wife time to put down her laptop and keys and to pour herself a vegetable juice before I told her.

"Mmm?" she said, holding my eyes.

"The same thing. Come and visit." This was third of her great-aunts to ring in the last month. I shrugged and leaned back on the lounge and smiled, but Tamara continued to look serious. Nothing significant in that---'serious' is her normal look.

"It's a campaign" she said; now she did smile, and she has a great smile. She came over behind me and bent forward and kissed me. "Have a good day?"

It's hard to say what a good day actually is in investment counselling. Well no, that's wrong, a good day---a really good day--- is when a client gives me the authority to handle lots of his money: more income for my employer and more bonuses for me.

I worked for my money though; employers in the 'hot' industries expect their people to put in the extra hours these days. I suppose I worked on average fifty hours a week Monday to Friday, but probably did four or five hours extra at home on weekends. It was *the deal*.

Tamara, as an events organizer, sometimes put in even longer hours. She worked more weekends than I did because a lot of the things she planned were held then. Theoretically she should have been freer during the normal work days, to compensate, but this did not often happen; she always seemed to be needed, which I suppose was flattering.

She was meticulous in her work. I sometimes went with her on a weekend to one of her events and was always impressed. She prowled around and checked *everything*; other employees took her queries very seriously.

Tamara earned almost as much as I did so we were doing well financially. We had bought a house two years before, just a year after we were married. It was more money than we had planned but the house was big and in good condition and in a very good area. We found we were easily managing the mortgage payments and in fact were now also thinking of an investment property.

We 'had it all' as they say, except for one thing---that small thing that we now both craved. Tamara wanted two of them and I was keen for three but although she had not taken the Pill for over a year we had so far been unable to manage even the first one.

We had had all the check ups and there did not seem to be any good reason. Tamara cycled regularly and all her systems were apparently ok and my little guys were good. We were *certifiably fertile*---but it was just not happening---and it was beginning to get to us. A bit.

***

"Have you got anything started for dinner?"

"As a matter of fact I have my darling, a lasagna"---a statement that would have earned an incredulous look from anyone who had known me only in my bachelor days, when I scarcely knew how to boil water. I had learned very soon after my wedding to a working woman that if I was to survive I would have to learn some culinary skills. And I had actually taken to it, even doing some night courses. Making a lasagna now was a breeze. "Can't you smell it?"

Tamara made a show of trying to detect it but gave up with a laugh and fell back against the cushions. "I'll make a salad" she said, but made no move to get up. She looked tired.

With her eyes closed she said "Melba will be next."

***

She was. I told the woman we would come up on the Saturday morning of the coming long weekend.

"In time for morning tea." It was a statement.

"Definitely." It would take less than two hours on the freeway from our suburb in Brisbane to Nambour.

"And you'll stay for two nights." Again a statement. I meekly said yes.

***

We had planned to leave our house by seven, so as to be ahead of the holiday traffic, but we had dawdled, and come eight we knew that if we started then we would be in the thick of it so we decided to wait until ten.

"I'd better ring" Tamara said.

"Why?"

"Well they're expecting us to arrive earlier."

"Does that matter?"

I was favoured with a fond look, as to a loved but slow learning child. "Darling, we are about to enter a different universe. Have you any idea what we are letting ourselves in for?"

"What do you mean? I've met the old dears. At the wedding---and I've been up there."

"Once. For an afternoon."

"Okay. I know they wanted us to stay overnight that time. And I remember all the food. They were very nice."

"Exactly. They *are* very nice. I'll have to stop them now preparing morning tea---which would have been several kinds of sandwiches and sweet scones and savoury scones and a slice and probably a cake."

"Good grief. Just for us?"

"For *any* visitor. But probably a bit extra for us. And I warn you, it'll be like that all weekend. You are going to lose that waist you are so vain about."

"I'm not vain......," but she had gone off to find her phone.

We did get going at ten and we still got caught up in the last of the traffic heading north but just past Carseldine it cleared and I was able to give the BMW its head.

***

Now---Tamara's aunts---actually her *great* aunts, sisters of her grandfather: Melba, Minerva, Harriet and Lily. All widows but, amazing as it might seem, all now living back on the same plot of land on which they grew up.

Their father had been the manager of Nambour's sugar mill and in 1920 had built a large house on six hectares of rainforest just on the edge of town. It was a quiet little place then but it's booming now---

lots of people moving up from the south. Those few hectares would be worth millions today.

The parents left the property to their six children, four girls and two boys; at the time they inherited they all lived elsewhere, in their own homes, but none wanted to sell the old home place.

When Melba's husband died she told her siblings that she would like to move back into the old family home. They agreed, asking no rent from her---but I understand she did pay something.

At that time Lily was living in Ipswich, where she had a dress shop. Her husband, who was considerably older than she, died the year after Melba moved back and she too decided she would like to return, and to build her own house on the land. Harriet and Minerva let it be known that if they survived *their* husbands they too would like to come back.

One of their brothers lived in Cairns and had fishing trawlers, and the other---my wife's grandfather---lived on the coast at Caloundra and had several small businesses in the town. The two men were much more comfortably off than any of their sisters and they deeded their shares in the property to them.

***

Harriet and Minerva were duly widowed and built houses on the land too, so for almost thirty years the four sisters had been living together at Nambour. Together but *not* together; their houses were only 50 metres apart, and connected by well trodden paths, but, as I recalled on my one visit, they were completely hidden from each other by the abundant trees and shrubs.

Four old widows, the *youngest* eighty one. (I forgot to mention that she, Lily, had remarried after moving there, to Larry who used to come twice a week to tend to the gardens. She was fifty three at that time and he only forty four---her 'toy boy'.)

This was the universe we were about to enter.

I realised as Tamara directed me to make the left turn out of the main street of Nambour onto the road that led to the aunts that I had totally forgotten the way; I think Tamara must have been driving when we came the previous time, which was just before we were married. As I followed the narrow road it did not seem at all familiar.

Within a minute Tamara said "that's it", pointing to at an open gateway ahead on the right, with the sign "Camelot" beside it. I turned onto a well maintained gravel driveway; it ran straight at first, beneath a canopy of big trees, before it curved to the left. It then curved right and then left again, taking us now into very deep shade, the trees pressing close overhead, but then we burst out into a sunlit clearing, with a wide lawn fronting a big Queenslander. *Two* big Queenslanders: a house fitting that description and beside it a tall woman in a wide straw hat: Melba.

As I pulled up she hurried towards us, and, I thought, surprisingly quickly for a ninety one year old. Arms were stretched out and Tamara was enveloped as soon as she stepped from the car. Then from around the corner of the house came the other three women and my girl was swamped. I was more or less ignored, but happy to be so. This was Tamara's moment; it was quite something to see the affection those women showed my wife.

After some interval they remembered their great-nephew-in-law and came at me. I did not get quite the same smother, but plenty of kisses and hugs just the same. As we were ushered towards the house an aunt walked on either side of Tamara, holding her hand.

***

Just off the rear of the big house was a gazebo shaded by a golden convolvulous. Under it was a big round table covered in a bright Gaughin print and it was obvious this was where we would be having lunch. A floral 'rope' had been looped from one support of the gazebo to the next, almost right around it. Tamara exclaimed, and made me look at it more closely. Two vines had been entwined and flowers had been threaded through them, so thickly that the vines were invisible.

"You didn't make this just for us? It must have taken an age" Tamara said.

"Harry did it."

"It's lovely Aunt Harriet."

"Thank you dear" she replied, and added "and while they're here you will call me Harriet!"

The others nodded soberly; I had the impression it must have been a regular demand.

We were offered a cool drink. It was a fruit thing of some kind but I couldn't identify it. It was obviously home made and had an unusual bouquet.

There was something else I couldn't identify---a scent---from some flower I supposed, as pervasive as tuberose but lighter. It seemed to be all around us. (I would learn later that it was an incense Lily concocts.) We did seem to have entered another realm.

After I had had a drink I went back to the car to get our luggage, and as I was walking back towards the group I was struck again with how much close attention the women were giving Tamara. One sat either side of her, holding her hand.

***

It was with some difficulty that we progressed through Melba's house to the room they had prepared for us, difficult because we were not in single file, all the women seeming to want to pass through doorways and hallways as a group. I kept well to the rear, with the bags.

Our 'room' was actually an outside porch, the fourth "wall" being the garden, with just a low rail between it and us. There was a big double bed, two cane chairs, a cane table, and a Silky Oak dressing table. A mosquito net was suspended above the bed, with the netting drawn back for the moment behind the bedhead. There was a rail attached high up on one wall with coat-hangers on it, and a lower one for, I guessed, towels.

I assumed the women would leave us while we unpacked, but they were not going to miss a thing. Two sat on the bed, either side of our bags, and two in the cane chairs. I hung some trousers on the top rail against the wall and Tamara unfolded a skirt and laid it on the bed. She had to move one of the pillows to do this and she said "oh" and held it up to her cheek.

"Feathers," Harriet said.

"And these sheets!" Tamara said, stroking them, " they're Egyptian cotton aren't they?"

"Yes" said Lily, and the women smiled at each other; she knows Egyptian.

"Oh, I could go straight to bed. Right now."

"Perhaps have your rest after a light lunch dear."

***

Light!? I have enjoyed many salad lunches---and have prepared quite a few myself now ---but *light* is not a description I could give this one. The food range was overwhelming--- and *everything* was tempting.

There were tomatoes of several kinds---tiny red and purple ones, and some that were green in colour but were actually ripe, and a big bowl of sliced "normal" ones, a bowl of separated crinkly lettuce leaves and another bowl of finely slivered Iceberg, large cucumbers sliced in a vinaigrette and tiny ones served au naturel, a potato salad plus little new potatoes that had been rolled in an oil or butter and sprinkled with chopped mint, platters of shallots and spring onions, some small dark things that looked like olives but tasted nothing like---more like figs, but actually not like them either---delicious anyhow---and some small round orange coloured chillies of which I was very wary at first but which I found produced only a pleasant warmth that suffused my whole body, almost like a drug. Everything was fresh and had lots of flavour, as if picked only ten minutes before. There were meats too, a tender corned beef and a ham, and a huge and still-warm damper.

Somehow my habit of eating little for lunch deserted me, and I surrendered it without a struggle. I caught Tamara grinning at me as I was hacking off another hunk of damper and could only grin back.

Our drink was the same one we had had earlier. They told us it was guava, but that bouquet......? I drank several glasses during the meal and I noticed Tamara did too.

With all the eating---and Tamara seemed to match me for appetite---there was plenty of talk. The women attended closely, not only to everything Tamara and I said but to what each *other* said. They were very alert.

Lily's husband Larry had appeared just before the meal, a very healthy looking seventy two year old, dressed in shorts and polo shirt and sandals, and very tanned. I had forgotten what a magnificent head of hair he had, a head of hair to make Bob Hawke envious, combed and swept back in that same style. Slightly oiled.

One strange thing---strange to me but not apparently to anyone else---was that Larry did not eat with us. After having helped himself to a plate of food he wandered off.

Half an hour later Larry reappeared and took platters and plates away, then returned with dessert---jelly, Spanish Cream, a tub of ice cream and a jug of pouring cream. He helped himself and once again went away. I had my share of those too.

Then Larry repeated his clearing routine and brought out a huge platter of fruit---slices of banana and pawpaw and melon and a sweet red grapefruit. I looked around at our hostesses in admiration.

"All from here dear" one said.

"All Larry's work" said another and I thought, this Larry is gold. After he brought out the fruit Larry stayed this time, bringing an extra chair. The women made room for him without fuss, as if that were the regular routine.

This 'light' lunch, which would have begun at about a quarter to one, did not finish until two thirty. The women did then allow Tamara and me to go off to our 'room'---where we threw ourselves on the bed.

"That was fantastic" I said. "I won't be able to eat any dinner."

Tamara giggled. "How about afternoon tea?"

"You're joking."

No answer; she snuggled into me and within five minutes we were both asleep.

I was awoken at three thirty by something tickling my nose. Tamara was using a feather that had escaped from one of the pillows. Sometimes when I wake from a short daytime nap I feel a bit irritable---a bit scratchy---but not this time. I felt as if I were floating on the surface of a warm pool, rested and refreshed. We smiled at each other and kissed, kissed quite a bit. There was nothing I would rather have done and nowhere else I would rather have been.

After a while though I became aware of sounds from within the house---footsteps, and the opening and closing of doors.

"Time to get up" Tamara said. "We're being given a message."

"Why? Lets stay here."

"I told you. Afternoon tea. Minerva's, at four o'clock."

I groaned again. "Surely not."

Tamara had moved to the dressing table, where she was brushing her hair. "Come on. You'll surprise yourself."

***

Melba led the two of us along a curving path beneath the trees to Minerva's house in another clearing. Harriet and Lily were already there.

"If you would prefer coffee…..?" but there was a big teapot on a wooden stand already on the table. "No, tea would be fine" I said; I felt that tea was the approved beverage for this ceremony at "Camelot."

On the table were two platters of little three-cornered sandwiches and two plates of scones, a fruit cake and little iced cakes and a big coconut slice. I was awed and a little panicked; could I do this justice? But I ate an asparagus sandwich then a savoury scone with butter then a plain one with jam and cream. They were all very fresh: delicious. The fruit cake won me next, and it was one of the best I have ever tasted---"we've made an extra one for you to take back"---and over my third cup of tea---and it seemed to be aromatic---I had a piece of the slice.

Questions were asked, directed mostly to Tamara---how did she manage a full time job and a house and cooking and looking after a husband? Tamara did her best to try to describe the day to day life of a modern urban working couple. The old ladies nodded and *seemed* to be taking it in but I was thinking how different all this was. For instance, there was just no place in our lives in Brisbane for such an afternoon tea, with all its preparations.

As it came to a close Harriet said "now what would you young people like to do? We've got a few ideas, but it's up to you."

I came in swiftly---I felt that I was in danger of being suffocated by all the attention. "Tamara and I would like to wander your paths and explore your woods." *Woods*; the 'other world' atmosphere was getting to me.

The others looked brightly at each other; "yes, lots we can show you there" seemed about to be offered so I continued. "Tamara and I have had no time together this week and it would be really nice to wander off on our own." I reached across and stroked Tamara's arm; I had to win this. "What do you think dear?"

Tamara played along. "That would be lovely."

The others might have been disappointed but they hid it well. As we walked to the steps off the verandah Lily said "remember, dinner is at seven o'clock. My place."

We took a different path from the one on which we had come, and as soon as we were around the first bend and out of sight of the house I stopped and leaned against the trunk of a large tree and held both hands to my belly.

"I can't believe how much I just ate."

"Me too. Its madness isn't it? 'Aunt madness'." We slid arms about each other's waists and walked on.

To look at six hectares of open grassland would take no time at all but these six were thickly timbered, and had slopes and curving paths; I thought we might get at least an hour on our own.

The first path brought us to the boundary fence and we decided to do a complete circuit before exploring the interior. On the other side of the fence the neighbours' lands were more or less cleared and because the aunts' property is elevated we had good views over them.

The first neighbouring paddock was pasture, kikuyu I think, with some tan coloured cattle; they had humps, and were very sleek. They were curious and very friendly too, coming right up to the

fence and allowing us to stroke them. Tamara thought they might
have become accustomed to receiving tidbits from Larry or the
women.

As we continued around we saw a grove of custard apples, then a
small lychee orchard, more pasture, the corner of a pineapple farm
and---we were now nearly back to the driveway entrance---some
more cattle. We continued along the road frontage and then back up
to our starting point.

We had seen a lot *outside* the property but looking into it we had
seen only vegetation---no houses---no sign at all that five people
lived here in four separate dwellings.

We decided to retrace our steps to Melba's and start our exploration
of the interior of this mysterious land from that point. Once there
we chose a path which we thought would lead us to Harriet's, and it
did. This was a cottage built in the same 1920's style as the original
house, but much smaller. There was a lawn, a well stocked herb
garden near the steps and a lemon tree---but no vegetable garden.
Harriet had returned by now and waved to us from the verandah.

From there we took another winding path and came to another
clearing and Lily's house, a somewhat bigger dwelling in a 1970's
style. Once again there was a herb garden and a lemon tree but
no vegetable garden, and once again its owner waved from her
verandah.

Lily called "if you go down there," pointing to a path that led off
behind the house, "you'll see Larry's garden. He's down there
now." A few more curves---I don't think there was a straight path on
the whole place---and there it was, and certainly worth the detour-
--rows and rows of vegetables growing across a gentle slope. Larry
was moving a hose from one furrow to another.

He told us that he had put down a bore not long after he and Lily
were married. "Good water, all you could want. I've got a three inch
main running right round the fence and I can tap in anywhere." He

held the hose out and we obliged him by taking a drink."Did you notice some cleared patches as you went around ?"

"Yes."

"They were my old gardens. I move every three years. It keeps everything healthy."

We stayed a while in this Eden; there were all the salad vegetables we had eaten at lunch, and a cornucopia of other things. "Before you go we'll come down here and you can pick whatever you want."

As we walked on Tamara said "he's a nice man."

"And happy."

"As we are,' and she slipped her arm through mine.

"This place is like something time forgot. It's---it's---mesmerising."

"Another universe."

"Your old dolls are like the witches in kids' fairy tales."

"Very *good* witches."

"Yes---and Larry is like their straight man, their connection with the real world. I thought at lunch it was a bit odd that he didn't eat with us. And he wasn't there at afternoon tea. I was wondering if he wasn't---I don't know---welcome?"

"It's not like that."

"No, it's not is it. I think he just---does as he wishes. He *prefers* to eat on his own. Maybe watches television somewhere---or bets on the TAB. I think if I were living here……." I did not finish.

"What?"

"Don't get me wrong but---living with these four women---I think I'd need a break too." I smiled as I said this, to take away any offence.

"I know what you mean. Oh---Lily told me---they are now *The Begums*. Don't you love it? 'The Begums of Nambour'. Mrs. Singh who has that big fruit shop on this side of town has decided to call them that. It could catch on."

We walked on, following yet another path. I could see that it, like the others, had been paved initially with a fine gravel but over time leaf fall had covered it, and now one walked on a soft deep carpet. We made no noise at all as we walked. A crow called from just above our heads, loudly, and we both jumped.

***

"Bring something extra to wear" Melba advised as we were leaving to walk to Lily's for dinner. "We are eating on her verandah."

It was so warm that the idea of having to put on a jacket or pullover later in the evening seemed ridiculous, but we heeded her words.

I could smell incense even before the place came into sight---and alongside the path for the last ten metres were tiny candles. They also lined the steps and the verandah railings. 'World' music was playing on a set somewhere---a reed instrument and whisper drums.

Our hostess appeared---in a long loose 'Indian' outfit, with lots of bangles and pendulous earrings. She wore silver sandals, her nails were painted, and she had an anklet with little bells on it. A Begum come to life!

I must have stood with a dumb look on my face because Lily burst out with a laugh.

"Melba, you didn't say anything…..? "

"No, I thought I'd let our guests have at least one surprise while they're here."

Just then the music changed to something with a definite Indian sound and Lily did some twirls.

"This is Lily's fun. We go along with it."

"Go along with it! You love it."

When the other two women arrived it was obvious that Lily's appearance was just as they knew it would be. They too had conspired to give us a surprise.

The hors d'ouvres were little curry puff balls, a spicy sort of dip---I'm afraid I don't know what was in it---and unleavened bread. These were followed by little bowls of another sort of dip and a huge platter placed in the middle of the table containing a couscous. We were invited to use our hands and were each supplied with a finger bowl.

Gamely we all did this and seemed to get the hang of it after a while. Some of us---me in particular---got pretty messy, but what made it worthwhile was the *taste*. Spicy---very aromatic---and very moreish. Or perhaps Moorish.

There were side dishes of colourful vegetables I couldn't identify and slices of banana and pawpaw with a tangy juice added, and a crumbly kind of bread that seemed to be all seeds. There were pieces of meat too and I tried and enjoyed them but because the light was so low---just the little candles---I couldn't tell what I was eating. It could have been goat's testicles.

Our drink was the ubiquitous guava plus a warm wine which I was told was made from rice but which was not Japanese sake; Lily said it was from Indonesia.

 It was a leisurely meal, with Lily exiting every so often to the kitchen to bring back yet another bowl or platter. Larry ate with us this time; he had in fact cooked many of the dishes.

He was a relaxed and confident host. He had not dressed 'alternate'---polo shirt and shorts and sandals again---but he had added this night a gold chain around his neck. Once again that great hair was perfectly 'set'.

This feast went on for hours. Things kept coming from that kitchen, the last course a lemony jelly-like dessert, with yoghurt; we were served coffee---strong and aromatic. And it did get just cool enough for the jacket---but not enough to prompt a move inside.

We did not get back to Melba's until eleven, where she said "now how about a nice hot chocolate?" Tamara and I both said no thank you together, and quickly.

"I couldn't handle a single thing," Tamara said, and Melba reluctantly put the saucepan back on the shelf.

So we went to bed. I should have been sleepy---I would have said beforehand that I *was*---but when we settled into that very comfortable bed, between those Egyptian sheets, I realised I felt very much awake. And with something else entirely on my mind. My wife it seemed had the same inclination.

***

I woke at six. I was on the 'outer' side of the bed and I just gazed at the garden as the light gradually strengthened. It was a cool morning but not so cool that I would not have enjoyed walking out into it in the nude, and I did think of doing that, but the realisation that our hostesses might come knocking at any moment stopped me.

A hand insinuated itself across my chest, pulling gently at the few hairs there, and playing with my nipples. The hand then slowly went on an exploration of the rest of my body. I was giving little whimpers of pleasure when Tamara said "listen". Low sounds were coming from the other side of our bedroom door. I made out receding footsteps.

A few minutes later---it was now just on seven---the sounds were back. Tamara giggled. Then we heard a tiny rattle. We both watched the handle turn slowly and then the door open a few centimetres. I could see very little at first in the dark vertical space but gradually I made out a pair of eyes, then *several pairs* of eyes, ranked above each other. I smiled and put one hand above the bed sheets and wriggled my fingers in greeting. With that the door was flung open and in they came, the last, Harriet, carrying a large laden tray.

"Good morning" they all said.

"Good morning."

"Did you sleep well?" Four bright pairs of eyes on us.

"Perfectly. Forgive us for not getting up aunts" Tamara said. "We're not wearing anything."

This did not seem to shock the old souls; if anything they looked approving.

"We'll just leave this here then" said Harriet, putting the tray on the dressing table.

When they had gone Tamara shimmied into her nightie and went to the dressing table.

"Don't tell me" I groaned.

"Oh you'll want to know. Pawpaw with lime, glasses of that guava drink---isn't it different? And u-n-d-e-r the covers---eggs and sausages and tomatoes. Oh, and bacon."

"God. What is it with this place. The food!"

"And toast and marmalade and a pot of tea."

"How do they expect....?" I began but I was handed a plate with some slices of pawpaw. They looked and smelled very tempting.

Tamara and I never had 'full' breakfasts at home but we fell onto this one as if it were our daily fare. We finished off all the toast and marmalade too and emptied the teapot---and it was a big one.

We dressed and joined the others under the gazebo. There---thank goodness---it was just talk, and good talk---the women were up to date on current affairs, and had decided views. But then it *was* off to Harriet's for a morning tea of pikelets and a fresh sponge. As those tea things were being cleared away the talk of the women was *about lunch*, which was to be at Minerva's; 'a light lunch' she said, but I was learning.

I forget what Tamara and I did next---laid down again probably---then it was over to Minerva's for pumpkin soup and fresh home made bread followed by a potato pie and a tuna bake *followed by* a lemon meringue pie with ice cream.

Of course you could say that Tamara and I did not *have* to eat everything, or *so much* of everything, but we did not seem to be able to stop ourselves. We had dropped our usual careful and light eating habits as easily as snakes shed their skins, and were wolfing our food as if we were farmhands just in from the fields.

We had a rest in our room after lunch but---since I am being very candid here---I have to say that, once again, we were in a frisky mood. We controlled ourselves however---there was the distinct likelihood that we would be disturbed---but we did manage a little discreet play---or foreplay for the night ahead.

Afternoon tea was at Lily's: scones and blackberry jam and whipped cream, and once again with everyone present. Larry partook but then went off somewhere with his booty---perhaps down to his beloved vegies. By now I well understood those self-imposed disappearances; those four elderly sisters were such a *force*.

***

Tamara and I did manage some respite from them that afternoon. We walked out the entrance of the property and up the road, climbing a long gradual slope to the west. I suppose we walked about three kilometres, and pulled up at a roadside lookout. From there we could see right back past Nambour to the east, almost to the sea. It was a beautiful view, and we could have sat and enjoyed it for hours.

I had difficulty in making out Camelot even from that height, but after a while I realised it was because I was looking for *houses.* The vivid patch of green just on the edge of town was in fact our temporary home.

We were sitting on a log bench. I had my arm around Tamara's waist---we were the only people there---and we kissed and I told her in some detail what I intended to do with her that night. Tamara warned me to be careful of what I was saying because if *we* could see Camelot then the aunts could see *us*, and if they had a *telescope* it could be trained on us at that very moment, and what if one of them could lip read? Such had been our experiences during the weekend that it all seemed possible.

***

Our final dinner was at Melba's. She does not have a separate dining room---all meals are taken at one end of her large kitchen. There are padded benches behind the table along two of the walls. If visitors were placed in the corners they would find it very difficult to get out. I think that if they weren't careful they could be trapped there *all day*, as one meal morphed into the next. It has probably happened.

Melba said it was to be a scratch meal---"we do that on a Sunday night"---but once again it could have fed a small village. We had the remains of Minerva's potato pie, plus a huge cauliflower gratin that emerged from Melba's oven, plus several types of green vegetables and then---something I had not had in a long while---a rice pudding, with extra cream. Tamara and I had double helpings of the pudding.

As we finished the pudding Lily said how about a game and the dinner things were whisked away and cards appeared. We played Five Hundred and---you don't need me to tell you---the Begums were bold and competitive. I was glad Tamara was partnering one of them and not me otherwise she would not have won a hand; that

I won a hand or two was only because my partner Minerva was so skillful.

After an hour it seemed that the women were just getting into their stride but Tamara and I---after exchanging those secret signals married couples manage---begged to be allowed to go off to bed.

From our bed we could just make out the sounds coming from the card game back in the kitchen--- but after a while we ceased to think about that.

***

Tamara gave birth two hundred and eighty days after we returned to Brisbane. A daughter, Lily Minerva.

I am still in the investment counselling business and doing better than ever but also busier too. Tamara went back into event organizing when Lily was six months old. That was supposed to be part-time but it is not working out like that. Our lives I'm afraid are hectic once again.

Lily is nearly two years old now and we have been trying for a few months for a sister or brother for her but so far no result. Then just yesterday Harriet phoned to ask us to come up on the approaching long weekend.

If it's a girl we are going call her Harriet Melba.

FIVE

THE RED SPEAR

The men struck a narrow river and followed it north; it was dry, with only occasional small pools, but eventually they did come to a large waterhole, over five hundred metres long, wide and shaded by Coolibah trees. One of the men dismounted and dipped his pannikin, drank, and declared the water fresh.

The party unsaddled, and unloaded their packhorses; their leader decided they would make the waterhole their base while they explored the land on the opposite side of the river---land which had not yet been taken up---which quite possibly had never even been visited by white men.

There was a large spear leaning against one of the Coolibahs. While the camp was being set up, two of the men were sent to circumnavigate the body of water, to see if there were any signs that Aboriginals were regularly using the waterhole. They reported seeing no ashes, nor collections of fish bones; there was just the one spear. It was similar to the spears they had seen being carried by Aboriginals they had come across in the previous weeks of their travels, except that it was considerably larger, and coated in red ochre.

The men used the site for nearly a month while they reconnoitred the land to the west of the river, marking out their selections. In their free time they caught an abundance of fish in the waterhole, but though they moved up and down the length of the waterhole they never saw signs of Aboriginal presence; the only evidence that other people had ever been there was the red spear leaning against the Coolibah.

There was something about it that caught the imagination of the men, whether because of its size or its solitariness. Certainly its colour always took the eye, especially in the late afternoon, when the ochre seemed to catch fire from the setting sun. At night it picked up the glow of the camp fire.

When the party left to return south after a month their leader wrote in his diary that the waterhole had been vital to their exploration. He named it Red Spear.

***

The men stayed south only long enough to pack their belongings and muster their livestock; they were anxious to return and claim the land they had selected. They found that their river had not yet been named---had not even been noted on the early maps. They began to refer to it as the "Ferguson", after the wealthy squatter who had helped finance their expedition. When a map of the area and the river was drawn by one of them he added the words 'Red Spear' next to the site of the waterhole. And when the men returned they found that the spear was still there.

***

Within ten years there was a settlement beside the waterhole---a few huts, a store and a shanty. The little 'town' itself became known as Red Spear. Remarkably its namesake remained in position against its Coolibah; something which had survived fires and willy-willys and storms was now surviving the arrival of the white man.

As the town took on a look of permanency the locals adopted the spear, even becoming proud of it. It lent their outpost, they believed, some distinction---a 'difference'. They were cross when they found that an official in a government office in Brisbane had decreed that the town would be known as 'Redspear'---one word. They tried to have this corrected but someone from the government wrote to say it was too late to change it.

Remarkably, no-one over the next forty years took or even moved the spear, even when the railway line came in the 1890s. At that time a bridge was built over the waterhole, and the whole town shifted to the western side, where the sandy soil was better for building upon than the black soil on the eastern side, which was unstable after wet weather. A low fence was placed around the spear and its tree, to give them some protection, particularly now from cattle.

As the years went by the artefact gained state-wide fame; all visitors wanted to see it. Strangely, local Aboriginals knew very little about it; they said it had probably been used for ceremonies. A visiting anthropologist wanted to take it back to the museum in Brisbane, but the locals would not allow it.

At the approach of Federation, with plans for building a Town Hall, a consensus grew that the spear should be housed there. It was placed in the foyer, attached horizontally to one of the walls. Today it is in the big new Civic Centre, upright, in a purpose-built showcase of glass and polished Ironbark, with a plaque at its base. All visitors want to see it.

***

The townspeople took it out recently and placed it once more against its Coolibah---which is still alive---when they had a Pioneers Day. There was a re-enactment of the arrival of that first party of men. Tapes of corroboree were sent from the Brisbane Museum, and played on an amplifier over the scene of the men setting up camp beside the waterhole.

The locals and the visitors watched the men taking possession of the site and the land. As the sun set that day the spear once again caught its light; some people said later, when talking about the day, that it was the spear they remembered most.

SIX

MY WESTERN WOMEN

My wife likes to tell friends---employing a literary reference---that when I go off to do my deliveries twice a week "he's visiting his 'Women of The West'." Well---two things about that---'west' is a stretch, because although my smallgoods run does take me in a westerly direction it is not really very far---just two hundred kilometres---and in this state that is nothing. The women of George Essex Evans' poem inhabited much more remote places; 'The everlasting sameness of the never-ending plains.'

And *my* women......? While most of my customers *are* women---and my wife knows I do have a strong appreciation of the better sex---none of them are remotely mine. I suppose though I have told her quite a lot about them, two in particular.

***

When we sold our advertising agency in Brisbane three years ago and moved up the coast, I was intending to do more fishing, and Jan to create her tropical garden. It's been good---we *have* done those things, and joined a film group and a very active bushwalking club, and gained some interesting new friends---but I found that I still wanted to have something to *do*, some regular work.

I wasn't thinking of buying into another business but I saw an ad for a part-time smallgoods run, complete with a refrigerated truck. I rang the owner; he was only my age but he said he had a heart problem and the work was now proving just too much for him. He had only ten regular customers on his run but was making a good return---and he thought it would be possible for someone to build it up further.

***

I do the run Mondays and Fridays. I leave at six, make the last of my deliveries in the town of Hartwood at the western end about one o'clock, have a break at Larsen's Hotel there for an hour and, with the straight run back, am usually home by five.

Larsen's is my biggest client and its owner is one of the women I have told my wife about. Laura Larsen has by far the busiest of the three pubs in Hartwood, and I think the reason it is so busy is that she has turned it into something much more than a drinking place. For one thing there are the *meals*; it's no wonder I deliver so much there because they do a tremendous amount of cooking, and not just at normal mealtimes. If you go there at any time of the day or night you will be fed. And *well* fed.

Also---rare these days---this is an *accommodation* place---and as it takes up nearly half a block, with three floors, there are a lot of rooms. There are two motels in the town, one at either end, but Larsen's seems to capture the travellers. Laura has told me that most of them are return customers.

The rooms are large and comfortable, the upstairs verandahs wide, with lots of easy chairs and lounges, the staff is attentive, the meals as I said are good and always available and the tariff is reasonable. Laura Larsen has 'got it down'.

***

Managing a business like that would be a lot of work, but that woman does it all on her own; there is no Mr. Larsen and, so far as I know, no business partner. She is certainly very experienced though; she told me she managed hotels on the coast for years before investing in Hartwood.

She would be I suppose in her late fifties---or early sixties---tall and fit. She is a decisive person. For instance, she deals with my invoices very quickly, and settles on the spot---though not before checking every entry.

Around the hotel she seems to be everywhere---not bustling, just efficient and businesslike---but for all that still seems to find time for a few words with everyone---guests, customers and suppliers like me.

All of the staff are women and like their employer they too work quickly and well. No request from a customer or a guest seems to be a trouble. The women are of all ages---predominately twenties and thirties, but some in their forties and fifties and a couple possibly even in their sixties.

I had thought I detected a *camaraderie* between them but it was not until my fourth or fifth visit that I learned that there was something to my feeling about this; one of the locals revealed to me that all the women are *refugees*---from unhappy marriages or, in some cases, domestic violence. Larsen's it seems is a haven for them---a steady job with a good boss---and even, if necessary, a home. If someone turns up with a baby, apparently a room becomes a nursery. I was told Laura Larsen never has to advertise for staff.

***

Laura was standing near my table one day while I was having lunch and I said "great hamburger."

"That's good---Judy's specialty. Can I get you a drink? On the house."

"Thank you, yes. Just a squash please."

"Mind if I join you? I've been on my feet all morning." She signalled to one of her girls and two squashes quickly appeared.

"I've been told about your Judys and Tammys and Cheryls. What you do for them."

She shrugged. "Well---I need staff."

"And some of these women need *you*."

"They need someone, that's for sure. But I don't do much really---I'm no 'Mother Teresa'."

'Well I think it's great."

She waved the compliment away, but with a 'thank you' smile. A thought struck me---wasn't there sometimes trouble---didn't the occasional angry husband or boyfriend turn up? Although she is a strong looking woman I doubted that she would have been able to eject someone like that from the premises. And there were no men on the staff. Did she ask customers for assistance?

"The police here are very helpful," she said. "Very quick to come."

When I told my wife about this woman she said she'd like to come out on the run and meet her. "I don't know though about your other one---that Abigail."

***

While working just the two days a week suited me I had thought I could still build up the business a little---fill up the run more. I called at the three service stations along the highway but did no good there---they were all tied to one of the big carriers. I had a little more luck with some shops in the two little towns along the route.

I did not try 'Abigail's,' a roadside café about fifty kilometres before Hartwood, because it seemed too insignificant. The café was set back about fifty metres from the road, half hidden by trees, and with a narrow insignificant entrance---how much business could the owner be doing? But after a couple of months it registered with me that there seemed to be quite an amount of traffic going in and out and I changed my mind.

***

There were no other vehicles there the day I pulled in, and I parked under a big Poinciana at the front of the café. The tree shaded both my truck and the wide front patio; there were several tables and chairs outside.

 The screen door squeaked as I opened it; the café was quite small, with just three more small tables with chairs, two tall glass fronted fridges on one side wall filled with soft drinks and juices, and a counter across the rear. There was no-one inside, but a sign asked customers to ring the little bell on the counter. I did, and then noticed a door in the wall behind the counter; I guessed that Abigail would emerge through that.

"Coming" said a deep voice, and shortly afterwards the door began to open. It is one of those swing doors and the newcomer was backing towards me, as if both hands were full. I saw a broad back and a thick neck. The figure turned and smiled---*a man*---with a round meaty face and a short thick nose that looked as if it might have been broken a time or two.

He was carrying a tray of sandwiches and he put it down on the counter. It was then that I noticed that he was wearing a *dress*.

I stammered out my name and why I had called.

"Abigail" he said, and thrust out an arm. To say his handshake was firm is to do it less than justice; it was just this side of crushing. Yet I don't think he was trying to impress---he was just so strong. "You go up to Hartwood don't you---to Laura's?"

"Yes. How do you know that?"

"Laura and I are mates. She rings me up for a yarn, or if she wants me for something."

He said he didn't think he could help me much because he had a little van of his own and he went down to the coast himself once every few weeks to get his supplies. As you can imagine though, I was finding it hard to give his words my full attention. The *dress!*

As he finished speaking he turned and *picked up a wig of dark hair* from a stand on a shelf behind him---I hadn't noticed it before---and plonked it on his head in one movement. It had a centre part, and swept straight down until, at about his jawline, it turned up and out a little. He did not adjust it or fiddle with it in any way, but he didn't need to; the thing had the rigidity of a helmet.

"Now that you're here how about a sandwich and a cup of tea?"

"Er---yes, good idea. Corned beef. Toasted thanks." I was mesmerised---I didn't want to leave without seeing more.

"It's nicer outside. I'll bring it out."

***

An old blue cattle dog padded round the corner and sat at my feet. A white cockatoo climbed down from a perch, waddled over to me and began to nibble the soles of my R.M. Williams. I waited impatiently for my next look at Abigail.

He came out first with the sandwich on a plate, telling me the tea would be a couple of minutes. In the open air he looked if anything even more robust. For the first time I noticed that he was wearing *women's shoes*, open toed, with some heel---I think they call them slingbacks---but he walked heavily in them. Surely they would soon collapse? No stockings---and massive calves.

The dress was bluish grey and rather fancy---silk if I was not mistaken---a cocktail 'frock', with a full skirt. It was tight at the top though---*very* tight; the man was fairly bursting out of it, his chest threatening to split the material.

It was all so incongruous. Under a bright and I daresay uncaring Queensland sky this muscular man---I suppose he was in his mid forties, but still very fit looking---*was wearing a dress.* No make-up, and no attempt to look or act feminine. It was *so* odd.

After he brought out the tea he pulled out a chair and sat---and as a man sits, legs casually apart. The dog went to his side and the cocky climbed up into his lap. He asked me how the run was going and suggested a couple of people I should approach. I told him about the advertising agency we used to have in Brisbane and why we had retired and moved where we had. But frankly my mind was whirling; how did *he* come to be here; what did the locals make of him; *why* did he dress this way (yet remain so unfeminine in look and manner)?

These were such personal matters that I held my tongue. I was sure that if I got to know him better over time I would learn.

***

He grew up in an inner Sydney suburb and did not do well at school; "I could have---should have---but no one in my family had ever stayed long at school, and I was good at sport." He played first grade rugby league for a few years. He was a tough player he said---and I could believe it---but all the time *he had an overwhelming belief that he was female.*

"I used to do all the things young men do. I had a succession of girlfriends, and had sex and all that, but I felt all the time---I *knew*---that I was playing a part. I was a fraud."

"Where did that come from?"

"I don't know. It started very early. Genetic I guess."

He got a job at a hotel---general hand, and 'muscle' when things got a bit rowdy---but in private he began to dress in women's clothing. When he turned forty he made the big decision to go bush, and there allow the person he believed himself to be to come fully forward.

Looking as he did, and settling in a rural part of Queensland, hadn't it made for difficulties? Weren't there reactions from the local graziers and their families? What about the inevitable rednecks?

"There have been a few moments. The 'necks' go away a bit sorry." I could imagine.

"And the locals…..?"

"Pretty good. Wary at first. Bit nervous. But people can't stand off forever. When I go down to your town now there're plenty here who'll look after the place for me for the day. Even when I take off for a break for a week or more." He grinned. "I don't go to dances though."

***

I learned in time that he prefers people to refer to him as 'she' but hardly anyone manages that. It's *his* fault---apart from the clothes there is nothing faintly feminine about him, in appearance or manner. He looks for all the world like one of those footballers on television sports programs who dress in drag for fun.

 And even if he did try to be more 'Abigailish', *could* he succeed? I can't see it; he's so obviously a *bloke*.

***

"Why 'Abigail' ?"

"Do you remember there was an Abigail in one of those early television series? She was independent. Gutsy. I admired her."

I have been tempted to ask what first name he went by for the first forty years of his life but I have refrained. I feel he would like to keep that to himself.

***

Last week I called in at Abigail's as usual for our chat and my toasted sandwich but he said that he had to go into Hartwood and because his van was temporarily out of action he'd like to come in with me. He probably wouldn't need to be there long he said so he could come back with me too. I wondered what he would wear.

***

On the few occasions that my wife has climbed into the passenger seat of my truck I have observed that it involves a *series of movements*. First she puts her handbag in---why women go everywhere with a bag defeats me, but there you go---then she makes sure of the positioning of her 'mounting' foot. Her left hand grasps the window edge of the door and she elevates herself slowly. As she settles herself there is considerable adjusting of skirt and other items of clothing. She turns the rear vision mirror towards her, and make-up and hair are checked. There is usually a restless moving of feet, accompanied by some comment about things that I have left on the floor. As I say, a sequence of small events.

Abigail flew up into the cab seemingly without touching anything---one could easily see the former athlete in the man. The dress on this occasion was a floral number with a lot of movement in the skirt---he does seem to favour the fuller numbers---but there was no adjusting when he landed---of anything. He sat there calm and still, quite unheeding of the ropes and tools that I tend to accumulate on the floor in front of the passenger seat.

***

As I approached Hartwood my mind was working. What business could Abigail have here? And did the citizens of the town already know this person, and his rather different mode of dress? I reasoned that he was probably going to see someone whom he knew well. Perhaps he would offer to come with me first on my rounds; wickedly I hoped so.

When the town came into sight I did ask him if he would like me to drop him anywhere in particular.

"You go to Larsen's first don't you? That's the spot." Ah, I thought, his business is there. I pulled in behind the big old hotel in my usual place. He said he'd be back in a minute; he just had to check in with Laura.

He returned very quickly and gave me a hand to unload. While we were doing it I noticed a number of the staff dawdling on the verandahs, and in the courtyard. Unusual; the staff at Larsen's never dawdled.

Abigail said he could not come with me to my two other customers and as I drove off I wondered what could be keeping him there.

***

When I returned just before one o'clock I looked for him---I hoped he might like to have some lunch with me---but though I walked through all the bars and the dining room I did not see him. I ordered a salad and went to sit at a table out on one of the ground floor verandahs.

I opened the local paper but had scarcely begun to read it when I heard a man's voice coming from the direction of the foyer. Then I thought I could make out Laura's quieter voice. The man spoke again, louder, and now in an angry tone.

I hurried along to the entrance. Looking in I could see the back of a strong young man, in singlet and shorts, facing Laura. Behind her was one of the younger staff members: Karen. I thought she looked frightened.

Laura's face was flushed. The man was shouting now, about his wife having to come home with him. He called Laura an interfering bitch. I decided I should do something---I wasn't sure what exactly---and moved towards the group, just as the man raised his fist in a threatening way.

At that moment a large floral object shot with great speed from Laura's office and hit the man from the side. There was no punch involved; it was what is known in football jargon as a 'strong hip and shoulder.'

The man rocketed across the foyer and hit the wall, back first, and slid to the floor, a look on his face of shock and disbelief. Abigail remained where he was, poised, legs slightly apart. He gazed at the fallen one without, it seemed to me, any emotion---quite calm, but definitely alert.

The man snarled, picked himself up and launched at his attacker. I am not sure of the exact sequence of events that followed---it was all so quick; there was a brief struggle then the singleted one was slammed onto his back.

The floor of the foyer is carpeted so I suppose his fall was cushioned to some extent, but not much I think. He lay immobile for a few seconds and then began to move his arms and legs---tentatively--- and without attempting to rise.

He was the only one of the five of us to make any movement. Actually there were now about ten of us---several men from the bar had crowded into the doorway, drawn I suppose by the noise. All of the standing remained motionless---it was like a tableau at an exhibition---Abigail centre stage, arms hanging by his sides, Laura with her arms held upward and slightly forward, Karen now with both hands over her mouth---and me just looking.

The young woman was the first to move, going to kneel beside the man and stroking his face. Laura looked at me and gave a silent 'gulp'; I moved to the man, who by now was making some attempt to get up onto one elbow. I really thought he might have needed an ambulance.

"Are you okay?" I asked as I attempted to help him rise, but he shook my arm off. He managed to get to his feet, very shakily, and, with the girl by his side, slowly made his way out through the entrance. Laura walked back to her office, grimacing at Abigail on the way. The gladiator himself looked at me, gave a shrug, and walked towards the bar door, the spectators scuttling before him.

At the door Abigail turned towards me. "Lunch?"

***

"So that was the business you had here?" We were seated back at my table.

"Yes. That geyser had threatened to come here at lunchtime today and get the girl. He works at the power station."

"Laura told me the police generally handle---that sort of thing?"

"Yeah, but the girl asked her not to get them. Bovver Boy's had a couple of run-ins before---apparently he's 'known' to them. She was worried he might cop a sentence this time."

"So Laura rang you."

"Yeah. I've had to do it once before. Same story---a girl---actually it was a woman about fifty. And---get this---she's back with him now. Laura says most of the girls are still soppy about their thugs. See that Karen?" He snorted. " Women! If *I* was a woman…." but he stopped there and grinned at me, and we both laughed.

Laura joined us, bringing three glasses on a tray. " My shout."

As we were about to drink Laura caught my eye and, half turning towards Abigail, raised her glass in a toast.

"I don't think we'll have any more trouble with that lad."

"You may have lost a girl though," Abigail said.

"I hope not---but anyhow, thank you," and turning to me, her glass still raised, "and thank you for bringing me my champion."

I raised my glass, and silently toasted the two of them. My western women.

SEVEN

HER HAIR

"Margaret?" She turned at the voice, to see the manager of the Home hurrying along the hallway towards her. "Have you seen your mother yet?"

"No, I just got here Bess. Anything wrong?"

"No, she's good. I think she'll make a hundred, that one. No---it's her hair---we'd like to cut it."

Margaret smiled. "And she asked you to speak to me?"

"Yes. Well---'the family'."

Margaret did not reply straight away, as if she were thinking.

"That's not a problem is it? It's just that with people in bed a lot of the time it's hard to keep long hair tidy. And there's the washing too, and the drying. The drying's the thing---it can take so long---and because they're old you have to watch out for colds and things......"

"Of course. We were expecting you to say something before now. By the way, if you think it's long now you should have seen it years ago."

"I did. I remember it---and she always put it up beautifully. She still does her hair in here."

"Yes, she will hate to lose it. I'll talk to her."

***

Tom had told Alice it was the hair that had caused him to fall in love with her. He had said that to her quite early in their marriage, and from then on had said it to lots of people. She told him if he kept telling people that they would think he was simple---but he never did stop.

She had been drying her hair in the back yard of her family home the very first time they had seen each other. He and his family had not long moved into her town from a property where he and his father had worked as stockmen. Tom had picked up a job at the railway and had started riding to and from the station on a pony.

Hers was a little town---one main street and only two more behind that, but there were lanes running parallel to the streets, at the backs of the houses. During the first week at his new job, when he was returning up the lane that ran behind her house, Tom had seen Alice in her backyard, seated on a log.

Her hair then was almost black, and very long---to her waist, thick and perfectly straight. It was lustrous, and caught the light. It caught Tom.

***

Soon Tom was giving her a wave as he rode his pony past in the late afternoon, if she happened to be in the backyard at that time---as she now frequently was. Her sister and his became friends at school, and Alice heard that he was telling his family about this beautiful girl with long hair that lived along their street. She didn't know what to think about the 'beautiful'---she didn't think she was even half pretty.

74

One Saturday morning, when her sister and Tom's sister walked into the general store where she worked, Tom was with them. She thought that, up close, he was quite good looking. Not handsome but---a *nice* face---good humoured---with smiley eyes.

Right there in the shop he asked her if she would be going to the dance at the hall that night. She said she didn't know, but both of the other girls said "of course she is."

For the dance she decided she would not plait her hair as she usually did when she went out but wear it semi loose. She tied two ribbons about it, one high and one much lower, and teased out the hair between, so that it formed a soft, full swathe. She twined some tiny yellow roses from their garden into it.

This night she did feel pretty. Tom claimed the first dance---a Gypsy Tap; he was a good dancer. He reminded her about the first time he had seen her.

"It was like you had the sun in your hair."

"Oh...." She didn't know what to say.

"I think you are the sun, Alice. *My* sun."

Crikey, she thought. She still couldn't think what to say, so she punched him on the arm.

"Ow!"

She was nineteen and he was twenty one.

***

When they married she moved in with his family. Tom and his father had converted a side verandah into a bedroom and a sitting room. They ate with the family and she helped with the housekeeping and washing and cooking. She found Tom's mother nice and his sisters were soon like her own---but she longed for their own place.

Six months on and Tom got a job as a delivery man for a produce merchant in a town a hundred miles further along the railway line. It was a much bigger town than her own and he was to be paid a much better wage. With some help from her father they put together enough money to get their own cottage.

***

She had kept her hair very long---Tom had begged her not to cut it---and for him she always washed and dried it outside, on weekends---when he was home---and on a bench that he had set up for her. He would sit with her.

At night he would watch from the bed while she took out any combs and pins and began brushing. He would prop himself up on the pillows, with a half smile on his face. "You look goofy" she would tell him.

She always put her hair into a single loose plait for bed. Sometimes he would leave the bed and take over the plaiting. He loved to do that---and whenever he did, she learned, he also wanted to make love.

***

In their new town, the one in which they would spend the rest of their lives, she noticed that her hair felt different. It was not so soft to the touch, and it didn't have the shine it once had. She mentioned this to one of her new friends at church and the woman said it was the town water. "I always use tank water----it's the only way." She mentioned this to Tom, and the next day a dray arrived in the lane behind their cottage with a tank on it.

***

The Depression---and in 1930 Tom lost his job, as many of the other local men did. By then though they had had Margaret, and she was carrying Susan. Men were leaving town, looking for work elsewhere; Tom decided not to leave his little family but to keep trying to find work locally. Because he was known as a good worker, and possibly also because he was well liked, he did get his share of whatever was going---but there were times when they had so little money she worried if they could carry on.

One day she heard that there was a man in town who was buying hair, at a good price. She went to the hotel where he was staying and he offered his highest rate, because it was so long.

She wrestled with the decision for days---she hadn't cut her hair for fifteen years. She knew how much Tom loved it---but right then they were going through a particularly tough patch. While he was out of town one day she went to the hotel. She was paid three pounds--- enough to feed the family for three months.

 She wrapped a scarf around her head when she left the hotel, not even taking it off when she was back in her house; to get the last shilling she had allowed the man to cut it very short. When Tom came home he was distraught; he wept.

That night as they were getting ready for bed she sat as usual in front of her dressing table but there was scarcely enough hair to run a comb through. He came and held her head in his hands and wept again. She told him it would grow again quickly but he made her promise never to do it again.

***

As it grew she knew that her hair had changed again. Whether it was the cutting or her increasing age or the struggle they were having she did not know but it was no longer straight, and when washed it went quite wild. Also, it was lighter in colour, and seemed thinner.

She still washed it only in rainwater but now found she had to use a little oil to make it biddable. She told Tom she would need to keep it shorter---just a few inches below her shoulders. She still brushed and plaited it at night, and sometimes he still did that for her; during the day she wore it up, in a bun or a roll.

Her daughters loved plaiting it for her at night, and watching her when she was putting it back up again in the mornings. She had only to say "I'm going to do my hair girls" and they would both rush to her bedroom. They would do this until they were old enough to leave home.

*****

Tom liked her to come and watch while he was 'creating' in his shed, particularly if he was working on something for the house, or for the girls. He was good with his hands, and had made many little toys for the girls when they were young.

One day she was holding a piece of timber that he was hand drilling and he asked her to move closer to steady it. She bent over it and just as he looked away at something a strand of her hair touched the drill. Though he turned it only twice more before her yell stopped him her head had been dragged right down to the bench.

It hadn't hurt, and in fact she started to giggle as Tom carefully and slowly reversed the drill and disentangled the hair. She thought it must have looked very funny, but her husband didn't even smile She went to wash the oil from the drill out of her hair. While she was standing in the laundry brushing it back into shape Tom came up behind her and put his arms around her and held her so tightly she could hardly breathe.

*****

As the years went by she thought at times how convenient it would be to have short hair---a bob or a perm as many of her friends had. She would mention this to Tom but she could tell he was unhappy at the thought, and she did nothing.

She did gradually shorten it---to shoulder length. She always wore it up when she went out though, usually now in a chignon, and still plaited it at night. In time it was the visiting grand-daughters who made the pilgrimage to her bedroom at night---and eventually great-granddaughters. In the mornings the little ones would attempt to pin it up for her again---but no-one could do it as neatly as great-grandma.

***

When Tom was almost ninety and becoming frail he went into the nursing home; he survived there for just a year. Two years later Alice was now in the same place, in the same room.

***

"Mum, Bess says they would like to cut your hair."

"Yes darling. What do you think?"

"Well, we'd be sorry to see it go---but if it really helps them...."

"Yes, it has to go." She laughed. "I'm not like Samson you know---I won't lose my strength."

"Susan and I will take a lock each when they do it."

"*They* won't do it. You two will."

***

The next day her two daughters went out with her into the rear garden of the Home. The manager had given them a dish and combs and scissors, and had arranged some seats and a little table in the shade of the Jacaranda in the far corner of the garden, just inside the back lane.

The cutting began, the two women working slowly and carefully, and in silence, but after a little while Alice said "come on girls, it's not a funeral", and soon they were joking and laughing, as the three had always done when they were together.

Some of the other residents, many of them old friends of Alice, came out to watch, and the manager brought out extra chairs; morning tea was brought down---fresh scones, made especially by the cook. There was a festive air.

***

She noticed the sound of hooves before the others did, and looked up. A young man was approaching up the lane on a pony. He pulled up at the sight---a semi-circle of old women watching another old woman having her hair cut; he thought it looked like a ceremony.

Alice raised her hand and smiled and he smiled and raised his hand in reply; after a few seconds he urged his pony forward and went on up the lane and out of sight.

EIGHT

GERALDINE

Because I live on a corner and have a lane at the back, as many allotments in country towns do, I have only one 'next door', but I am very fortunate to have those particular neighbours--- Rod and Geraldine and their two boys.

Rod Dutton works at a mine that is about half an hour south of us. (We have quite a few coal mines dotted around this part of Queensland). Rod is not at manager level---he refers to himself as a 'dogsbody'---but he seems to have a lot of responsibility, and I would say is paid well; the couple have all the latest conveniences in the house, and two newish vehicles, one of them a four wheel drive, and their last two family holidays were overseas ones. Rod is certainly a good 'provider'.

Geraldine does a little work at the Council office and also helps out at the school as a teacher's aide occasionally, but she is mostly at home. I too am home a lot of the time, as the result of the managers of my businesses doing their jobs rather too well, so I see more of her than I do of Rod. She will join me on my verandah for a cuppa or I will be called over to try a cake or some biscuits she has just baked. We talk freely then; she is not only an outgoing person but, with me at least, extremely candid. She's good company for a widower whose kids have all grown up and left home.

Rod is more reserved but he and I do have good talks, when we share a beer down the backyard. We do this perhaps once a fortnight, at the place where our fence is lowest and where their two boys climb over whenever they want to play with my chooks, or kick a football around, my yard being much larger than theirs.

Rod and I park ourselves either side of the fence in a couple of old deck chairs under the big Poinciana there. There is a little weather-beaten table against the fence on his side and we rest our stubbies on that. Geraldine will come out with some nibbles but generally doesn't stay long, if it is late and she is getting dinner ready, or trying to get the boys under the shower.

Rod and I tend to talk 'serious'---the big issues you might say; we sort out a lot of the world's problems under that Poinciana---but one afternoon recently he was in a merry mood when we met.

"Gerry's just told me this. There's this woman she knows---hubby's put on a lot of weight---let the whole personal hygiene thing go too---not showering enough---that sort of thing. Anyhow she asks Gerry what she should do. She's nagged this geyser silly but hasn't got anywhere. Gerry says---get this---'fight fire with fire'......"

"You mean....," but I thought I knew what was coming.

"She says to the woman---do the same! Well, this is gonna be hard---she's one of those immaculate women, you know---keeps the house the same way---but she's desperate." Rod took a hurried drink. "Anyhow she starts to let the dishes pile up, and the washing. When our boy's getting ready for work there are no clean clothes---and if there are, they aren't ironed. The heap's a metre high. In the lounge room!

When he comes home the beds haven't been made. And *she's* a mess---hair not done, daggy trackies---you know. Apparently she smartens up if she goes out during the day---this is just in the house.

She's told her close friends what she's doing---told them not to call for a while."

"Looking horrible just for him?"

"That's it. Anyhow it's a couple of weeks before he says anything and then she throws it right back. "Why should I try anymore? Look at you!"

"So how long…?"

"Only another week! Tarzan starts to get his act together---showers every day---has a haicut---loses some weight---smartens up all round. She reckons everything's back to normal now."

He leaned back, beaming. "So isn't my wife a clever girl?"

I could have told him that the woman is cleverer than he realises.

***

As I said, Geraldine is very open and candid with me---even telling me quite personal things about Rod and their marriage---almost embarrassingly so at times; I might be some sort of father confessor figure for her, I don't know.

I wrote a story following one of her 'confessions'. Never be able to show it to her of course, or anyone, but I enjoyed doing it. I called it......

A WOMAN'S WORK

"I've asked Greg and Belinda over for lunch tomorrow," Rod said, "barbeque." And she and Deidre were planning to take the kids to the free concert the Council was putting on in the park.

She said nothing in reply but walked quickly from the lounge room out onto the verandah and sat on the daybed there. This had gone on long enough---from right back to when they had got married. Really from before that. It had to stop.

She had gone straight from school at seventeen into an office job; McClintocks was the biggest law firm in their town and Bert McClintock, who was a friend of her father, had always said that she could have a job there. She had saved quite a lot of money from part-time work while she was at high school and had had half a plan to travel overseas with one of her friends but her father had dissuaded her. "You should get some real work under your belt first. And you'll get on well at Bert's---he likes you."

She had given in---and found she had liked the work, and the people there---and then within a year she had met Rod. Her father had thoroughly approved of him; "he's got a good head on him. He'll do alright." Rod had a job at a mine, and people told her he was well thought of there.

One of the things that made Rod attractive to her was what she thought of as his *maturity*. She liked the calm and authoritative way he had of making decisions, *and for both of them*. It was *he* who decided what they would do on the weekend---whether or not they would go to a particular dance---even sometimes which dress she should wear. "I don't like that one. Wear this one."

When they married she was only twenty, he twenty two, and Rod became, as she knew he would, the dominant partner in their marriage. *He* decided when and where they would take holidays---what kind of car they would buy--- what colour they would paint the house---even when they would start a family.

She never resented this, not even when friends ribbed her about it, but she did begin to think more about it after they had had their first child. What effect might Rod's ways have on *him*?

Rod himself had been an only child, in a household where the father was quiet and mild mannered, not forceful in any way. She had grown to like her father-in-law, and to respect him as a decent and principled man, but she saw that he did readily defer to others;

it was easy to understand how his son by contrast had grown up so assertive and confident. But what effect would his manner now have on their own son?

By the time their *second* boy was a few years old her fears about this had evaporated. The boys had worked out their own ways of manipulating their father---as most children do---but there was now the effect it was having on *herself*, particularly the assumption by Rod that she had no plans or ideas of her own, or that if she did, he did not need to consider them.

When he had said recently that it was time to paint the house again, and white---and she had said that she had been thinking of a warmer colour---his response had been to merely look at her, and with a puzzled sort of expression, as if he were thinking not so much about her idea but *the fact that she had expressed it*. And then he had said no, white was best.

She had gone along with it, as she had with everything; "I've booked us into Brampton Island at Christmas---I'm going to cut down the Jacaranda---I think we'll buy that block next to the Davidsons........."

She had not made an issue of anything---but why did Rod always assume that *she* had no useful ideas---and why, like now, did he assume that she never had any schedule, or plans? Just that morning he had said "we'll go out to the dam this afternoon"---a good idea, it was going to be very hot again, and the boys would love it---but couldn't he ask her if *she* had anything in mind? Did he think that she *never* thought ahead, from one day to the next---even from morning to afternoon?

Now this barbecue announcement. No---it was time.

***

"Something up?" Rod asked when she walked back into the lounge room.

"No, I---just remembered where I left a sewing needle." A little lie, to give herself a moment. She found her heart was racing; why was this so hard?

"Anyhow honey, a barbecue lunch tomorrow with the Pratts?"

"Look I can't. I'm going with Diedre to the concert with the kids. I was hoping you might like to come?"

"When is it?"

"It starts at twelve."

"It'll go all afternoon. This is just lunch. You can go later."

"Darling, you know Greg and Belinda. They *never* want to go home."

"But---you like them." It was a statement, but with the hint of question.

"I do, but this concert will be great. Ask them for *next* Sunday." Her mouth was drying. She hurried out to the kitchen but found she hardly knew what she was doing there. When she went back through the lounge room Rod was reading the paper. Was that a frown? A few minutes later though, from in the kitchen, she could hear him on the phone to Greg Pratt. Yes!

***

A few afternoons later Trevor Springer came to the door.

"Trevor" she said, with she hoped no hint of welcome in her voice. She thoroughly disliked the man.

"Hello Gerry. Rod out the back?"

"Yes. Go through."

When she looked from the back verandah after a few minutes she could see the two of them drinking beer under the Poinciana. A little later Rod came up and asked if she was going to join them.

She exploded. "No! You know what I think of that man!" A man whose attentions to the daughters of her friends were insensitive to say the least, almost molestation. She knew other things too; the man was a pig. "How could you ask him here?"

Rod had looked blank and in a flash she realized that he had never taken any notice of her opinions about their visitor.

"You did say something darling, but…"

She cut him off. "Does what I say mean *anything* to you?" She picked up her car keys. "I detest the man. I'll be at Melanie's. Phone me when he's gone."

As she drove out the gate she had glanced back at the house; Rod was still standing at the front door, looking after her. When she returned close to dark he had said nothing but gave her a long hug.

***

With the hug she thought she might have been getting somewhere, but a few days later he said "we'll go over to the coast next Saturday. See Mum and Dad."

She lost her temper. "How about *asking* me Rod?! Why don't you ever think that I should have some say in these things?" He stared at her. "*I* might have something planned."

"Have you?"

"No! But you didn't know that!"

"You would have told me."

"Yes I would have. No---I would have talked it over with you---not *told* you."

He was frowning. "Look, we don't have to go. I just thought ---it's been a while since we went. You enjoy seeing them."

"I do darling, and yes, let's go." Dear God, she thought, this is going to take a long time.

***

The next day, after Rod had gone to work, she took the phone off the hook, made herself some coffee and went to sit in the lounge room. I'm smart, she said to herself, I will work this out---but it took more coffee and a couple of hours and a lot of walking around before she came up with the answer. *An* answer anyhow.

It was quite a simple one. If she was going to get her husband to talk things over with her then she needed to make a big point of *discussing her ideas with him.*

"I was already doing this Hugh," she told me. "I'd always done it. I liked to hear what he thought. I liked that feeling of---partnership. But he *never* did it with me. I realised that what I had to do was make what I did more obvious."

"*Condition* him?"

"That's it. I thought---this would work if someone did it to me---it should work on him. But, oh Hugh, I knew it would take a long time. I'd read that the big ocean liners like the Queen Mary actually take ages to stop. Rod would be like one of those. I didn't want to stop him though---I just wanted to turn him. A bit. Like a little tug."

"Toot toot! I'm beginning to shift my sympathies. Rod never really had a chance."

"Oh yes, poor *Rod*. You men! What about poor me?"

We were in the easy chairs on her verandah. I smiled at this confident woman sitting opposite me. "Someone should have warned him" I said.

A peal of laughter. "Yes---but it did take ages. I couldn't believe after a while that he wasn't getting it."

"How long before you did notice some 'coming about'?

"Three months."

"That doesn't sound too bad."

"You don't know the effort this little tug was putting in! But once I started, it was---a challenge. Some women take up a hobby and this was mine---and I was deadly serious."

"Do you remember the first.....?"

"Never forget it. It was right here. We were sitting just like this." She raised her eyes. "Forgive me darling."

I raised my right hand, as if making a vow in court.

"That's alright. He probably tells worse stories about me at the club. Where was I? Oh---he was having a beer and I was drinking---something---and *he asked me if I had any ideas about where we might go for our next summer holidays!*

Hugh, that might not seem much to you---from what you've told me about your married life that would have been normal---but this was the *first time* Rod had ever asked me something like that. I was overjoyed---it was one of *those* moments. Where did *I* think we should take *our* next holidays?"

"Was that how it was from then on?"

"No. I had to keep it up. But it was the start---and it's got better and better."

THE END

A day after Rod had told me about his wife's success at helping another woman influence *her* husband I was handing Geraldine some eggs over the side fence. "Rod reckons you should become a marriage counsellor."

"He did?" she said, then caught my look and laughed. "Oh, that couple. Yes, that was a great success. But I've actually got my next client."

"Oh?"

"Timmie. He's becoming difficult. With me anyhow. Aggressive. Using *rude* words."

"My Nick did that. It's a phase."

"Yes, well, it's going to be a short one."

As she disappeared back inside the house she called "toot toot."

NINE

JANUARY

She kept glancing in the rear vision mirror as she drove down their street, but her mother was not looking. Even as they had been walking down the driveway together her mother had swept at things on the concrete, stopping once to deal with an errant bougainvillea shoot. Helen had been barely behind the wheel of her car before her mother had spotted something in the lawn and dropped to her knees.

Helen kept her arm out of the window and was still waving when she reached the corner but her mother had still not looked up; her father had long since walked back up the driveway.

Waving was not over though; there was her friend Lesley with her two little daughters at their front fence. Helen slowed and put her head right out of the window and called goodbye. The girls danced and waved for their lives and Lesley looked into her eyes and mouthed something that could have been 'good luck'. Then she was past.

It was a shame that the two had become friends only recently; they had met first when Helen had been walking Skip, and soon Lesley and her girls had been joining her on the walks. She had never met the husband.

As she neared the next corner she looked in the mirror and saw that Lesley was still standing at the fence. Helen waved one last time and turned onto the main road. Goodbye friend.

"Your father says the only way to go is up to Fraserfield first" her mother had said, "so you could stay with the Hatfields."

The short journey into the city and over the Story Bridge was so familiar to her she often completed it with no recollection of its little events. And today it was not until she was half way across the bridge that she reminded herself that this would be her last time. I'm crossing my bridges she thought---heading for a new life. She looked across the river at the city centre: goodbye Brisbane.

Soon she would be passing the sugarcane on the flats beside the highway, with the banana and pawpaw plantations up on the hillsides behind. She knew this early part of the trip too; she had travelled it once a week or once a fortnight for the past two years.

***

It had been a real disappointment that her first teaching post had been so close to Brisbane. She had wished for a distant town, small and isolated, in the Gulf perhaps or the Far West. She had told the Department she was happy to go anywhere in the state---had told her family and friends that she would soon be far gone. She'd taken pleasure in their expressed alarm and admiration. Then, Booroolgan---her father sometimes drove further than that on a weekend to go fishing!

Her mother had remembered that the Harrisons lived near there, so at least she'd know somebody. "You used to be very friendly with their girl." Who had since become very religious, and with whom Helen had now really very little in common.

She had thought she would hate the place but it had been good. The kids had been a nice bunch, friendly and well-mannered, like the other country children she'd taught during her training. Their parents had been very supportive and the family she'd boarded with had been as nice as pie.

It hadn't been their fault that she was turning away from that. Though she knew she was competent---and she did like children---it was the job of teaching itself that she no longer wanted.

"Well what then?" her mother had asked in their lounge room---but Helen had not known. She remembered looking at her mother and thinking---tell me Mum. Tell me something about myself---just this once---something only you could know. Instead she heard "have you talked to your father?"

"Mum, when you were twenty-two didn't you dream of getting out of that office and doing something else?", but she had been machine-gunned with "when I was twenty-two I was engaged to your father and we were saving every penny we could," and then the woman had remembered something she had to do in the kitchen.

Helen had once walked into the lounge room when her mother was demanding of her father that he 'speak' to her, and she had tried to get both to talk. But her mother once again had had 'other things to do'; her father had asked her if she knew what she wanted to do next, and when she'd said 'no', had seemed to lose interest.

Another time, when her mother had been on the phone to Helen's eldest sister, and in full cry on the subject, Helen had deliberately walked into the room. Her mother had not changed the subject; "I mean, if I'd had the advantages this young lady has been given"---flicking her eyes towards Helen---"I think I'd have had the sense to use them", but she didn't want to talk to Helen after the phone call.

Her father remained as he always had been with her, unperturbed. Not censorious, but not really curious either. He had never been curious about her; it was as if his youngest had no power to surprise him. For as long as Helen could remember her father had just nodded and accepted every piece of news he heard from and about her.

It has always been easy for her to get her way at home. If, as a child or teenager, she had told her mother about something she wanted to do and her mother, even if she was against it, had told her husband, he would say, "well, if that's what she wants," and that was the end of it.

Helen had often wondered about that; she was the fourth and last child, all girls. Was she actually the son? "Don't be silly," her mother had said when she'd once voiced the thought. Whatever it was, she had been treated differently. She had wondered more than once if they really loved her...

**

She had studied 'Positions Vacant' in the "Courier Mail" from midway through the year, but nothing had appealed. There had been some jobs in the Public Service which her teaching qualifications might have allowed her to get, especially if she had been prepared to do more study---and she would probably have had no difficulty in arranging a transfer---but she applied for none of them. Then, in the same week in November that she put in her resignation, she bought a copy of "Queensland Country Life" and saw there an advertisement by a businesswoman in a western Queensland town who wanted someone to rejuvenate her hotel and the businesses attached to it. Not at all what she had had in mind, but the last line of the ad had attracted her: 'Experience not necessary, but must be smart'. It was old-fashioned wording and she knew she often clicked with older people. Parents excepted. And she believed she *was* smart.

**

Home was half an hour behind her and she was now amongst the cane. Fraserfield lay due north, but the turn-off to the alternate road west over the range and through the Burnett was coming up. Which way? She hadn't phoned the Hatfields; she took the turn, and almost immediately the road began to climb.

Twenty minutes later and she was descending into a valley. The rains of summer had not yet arrived and the hills were brown, but on the flats the irrigated lucerne and sorghum and maize engulfed her in all shades of green. There were herds of Australian Illawarra Shorthorns and Jerseys, and here and there a tractor, someone cutting hay or carrying irrigation pipes. Nearly all the sheds were unpainted, and some of the houses too. Helen had seen houses like that on the edges of cane fields at Booroolgan and she'd thought them abandoned till she'd seen washing on the line or children playing.

In the main street of the valley's little town there were no people in sight and only one vehicle, a small truck. It was parked in front of a little convenience store and Helen decided she too would stop, for a drink. She drew in beside the truck, and as she got out she found herself looking into the big eyes of a young calf. There were other calves, perhaps twenty. She stood closer, and as one put its nose between the wooden slats she offered it a finger. It started to suck and its dark eyes closed in contentment. With her other hand she stroked the soft hair on its neck.

"Looks like you've got a friend." The speaker was a woman, middle-aged with bushy brown hair showing a few streaks of grey---no make-up, a singlet, baggy shorts and gumboots. Behind her stood a man, also in singlet and gumboots. They both carried ice-creams.

"Are these yours?"

"Yes, curse them. Would you like one?"

"Or all of them?" asked the man.

"What's going to happen to them?"

"We're taking them home. We feed them."

"We?!" the woman snorted, and dug her husband in the ribs. The man recoiled and nearly lost the ice-cream from its cone. Helen and the woman laughed and the man retired to safety, to lean against one of the shop's verandah posts. The three smiled at each other. A calf called for its mother.

Helen learned that Doug and Shirley had a dairy farm on the flats, but their house was up in the hills on the far side of town, and they were taking the calves there to rear them.

"And what about you dear?"---and she began to tell them where she was going and why, talking easily in response to their frank curiosity. Time slipped past.

Helen felt sorry when the man said that they'd better get going. "But let us know how you get on. We're the Wilsons by the way." As the woman was about to climb into the cab, she hurried back and hugged her. "Good luck love."

As she watched them drive away up the main street she felt sure they'd be talking about her and she wished she could eavesdrop. As she sipped her drink, sitting on the bench under the shop awning, she began to feel for the first time that day the weight of what she was doing. Her new home was over a thousand kilometres away from Brisbane; would she make friends there? What if the people were too different? She allowed herself a minute of unquiet over the thought then pulled herself out of it; they might all be like Shirley and Doug.

As she began to climb the winding road that took her up out of the little town, she glimpsed the little truck far up ahead, almost at the summit. I won't catch them, she thought. But when she reached the top they were there beside the road, at the entrance to a driveway that led up to a house and sheds. Doug was at the wheel reading the paper and Shirley was leaning on their gate; oh, they waited for me. She tooted and waved and they waved back and then she was past.

A favourite song began on the car radio and she hummed along. The road wound before her now to the north, and through gaps in the trees she could glimpse a valley ahead. She smiled to herself but then her throat closed and tears came.

What was this? She wiped her eyes and told herself not to be silly--- this was an adventure. She was lucky; she was *happy*.

TEN

PEARL

"The kids keep on at me to write up my story---my life," I tell the old woman.

She is sitting up in her bed at the Home. "Yes do that dear. You've seen a lot of changes. The young ones today have no idea what life was like when you were young."

And far less idea of what it was like when *you* were young, I think. One of the reasons I have put off writing about my own life is because I don't think it is that interesting---suburban solicitor--- living in the one city all my life; I have been much more of a mind to do *hers*. Or combine the two. I tell her this now.

She thinks about this for a moment---or perhaps just 'goes away', which happens frequently now, though she always snaps back---and invariably takes up where she or we left off. She nods. "And call it 'Family'. Where would you start ?"

"Well, I suppose I should begin when you were born."

"Yes," and then she chuckles, and a wizened hand moves across and grasps my arm. "Just don't begin the day we met!" We both laugh--- but I think if I were writing a novel---or the screenplay for a movie--

-that would be a good place to start. What hostility, what aggression I met with that day; if looks *could* kill, my life would have ended right then.

***

Pearl was born in Melbourne, in 1916, while her father was fighting in France; he was killed there the following year. In 1919 Pearl's mother died in Melbourne in the Spanish Flu pandemic that swept the world. So, at age three, she was an orphan.

 Her mother's mother looked after her for a year, but she herself was in poor health and found she could not manage an infant. No other relative came forward to take her and she was placed in a church run orphanage.

Pearl told me she was happy there---that it was a good place, with caring friendly staff; perhaps it was somewhat of an exception, when one hears the horror stories that are coming out today about some of those institutions. The only unhappiness *she* recalled was when she saw other children being visited by members of their families; in all the time she was there she never received one such visit.

Pearl told me she thought that that probably affected her to some extent; "I think I always was a 'serious' child, and possibly this made me more so. More reserved you might say. But I was a romantic inside you know; as I grew up I dreamt of having a handsome husband and lots of children."

***

When she was seventeen she was accepted as a trainee nurse at one of the big hospitals in the city. She excelled at her work and her studies, she told me; "people said I had a gift for nursing---that it was my 'true vocation'.

There were quite a few older nurses there that hadn't married---and in those days if you did get married you had to leave the job anyhow---but I 'knew' I would get married one day. I didn't tell anyone this---kept it to myself."

***

Another war now and another city---Brisbane, in 1942; the couple who will become my parents meet at a dance in the inner city suburb of Fortitude Valley. There are many soldiers in the city at this time, and public dances draw big numbers of them. Brisbane's girls flock there too.

Thea is twenty, and works as a typist in the office of Patterson's, a big department store in the Valley. Charlie, twenty-three, is in the Infantry; he and his fellow soldiers have been told they will soon be sent into action; they think it will be in New Guinea.

Charlie is tall and solidly built---"a country bloke," Thea will one day describe him to me, "but not a shy one." She is slim---vivacious---and considered by her friends to be 'bold'; "I chose my partners, and asked *them* to dance."

The night they meet there are more soldiers than ever in the hall, and they stand two deep along the walls; when Thea first notices Charlie he is in the back row. It is his height that first draws her attention, but she likes his blond hair too, and then she decides that he is actually quite good looking. When he talks to another private beside him he smiles a lot, and she likes that too.

'Bold' as she is, she cannot bring herself to push past one line of men to ask someone at the back to dance, but the band starts to play and the first line surges towards the girls on the other side of the hall and she has her chance. She walks quickly towards him, catches his eye, smiles and lifts her arms a little and he moves towards her.

At the end of the quickstep she thanks him and moves back to her friends, but two dances later he is standing in front of her again. They dance and talk together for the rest of the evening.

***

She is a girl from suburban Brisbane who left school at fifteen, as most of her friends did, and after a short secretarial course had got the position at Patterson's.

He had been brought up on a large sheep property out west, where his father was the manager. He had been schooled at home until he was ten and then went to the town of Charleville where he boarded at a hostel. He tells Thea that in his teens he was often asked by his teachers to help some of the slower ones in his class, and often spent more time on *their* homework back at the hostel than he did on his own.

After leaving school at fifteen he had begun working as a stockman on stations in the district, and was overseer on a very large one when he joined up.

Thea would tell me one day that she thinks she actually began to fall in love with him when he was telling her about helping the other children. She laughed when she told me that, as if to say to her teenage son that she was half-joking, but, thinking about my mother's quick responses and somewhat impetuous nature, I think it was probably true. And he had a good voice she said, soft and clear---and that nice smile.

***

Charlie Wheeler makes her promise to come to the next mid-week dance; on the tram ride home the other girls tease her about her new 'beau'.

On the Wednesday night they dance only with each other. They arrange to meet on the Saturday, at midday in the Botanic Gardens.

"I was nervous. Would he turn up? I mean, it's one thing to have a good time with a person at a dance---that's why you're there---and it's night time---you're all dressed up, but this was days later. Things are different in daylight.

And---you young people mightn't understand this---I've seen you at the school when I pick you up sometime, boys and girls all milling around together---you're all so easy with each other these days. It wasn't like that in the Forties. I was nervous.

Anyhow, I got there early, and I was sitting on a bench in the Gardens near where we said we'd meet and then he comes through the gate and along the path towards me. Strolling along as if he hadn't the slightest doubt I would be there.

You know, Charlie wasn't cocky---you wouldn't say that---but he had this *confidence*. Trust really---as if he *trusted* people to do what they said they would. I said I would be there and there I was. And of course he had that big stupid smile on his dial."

They have lunch there, then walk to the pictures---as they were called then---arm in arm, and see a matinee. There my future mother and father share their first kiss.

The romance grows quickly; Charlie meets her parents and they like him. Then, with only two day's notice, the order comes for his Company to move north. Thea persuades a friend to relinquish her flat, so that she and he can spend one night completely on their own.

Charlie is fairly certain they are headed for New Guinea, but so are the Japanese. He could be wounded---he could be killed; they know that this might be the last night they will ever have together. The realisation sweeps reserve away, and they make love.

***

Charlie leaves Brisbane on a packed troop train. A month afterwards Thea and her parents learn that a ship has been attacked and sunk just off the coast of New Guinea. No more letters are received from Charlie. The only information they can get from the Army is that Charlie has been reported as 'missing in action'.

Thea tells her parents she is pregnant. Her mother tries to persuade her to go 'on holidays', to her Aunt Hilda in Sydney, but she refuses---she is not ashamed of her condition. She knows that her parents want her to have me adopted but she will not agree to that either; "what if your father had survived?"

***

By the time I was born her mother and father had come around. Thea and I lived with them; she got a job in a war clothing factory and my grandparents looked after me during the day---and from what she told me later, dotingly. My grandfather, himself a World War 1 veteran, was retired from his bank job by then, and apparently there was almost a competition between him and my grandmother for my attention. I was in very good hands.

Thea continued sending letters to Charlie, writing mostly now about young Raymond Charles. These letters went to the general army postal address, but the only replies were repeats of 'missing in action'. There must have been many such messages going into homes during the war; I can only imagine how awful that must have been.

***

Thea liked her work place, a small factory with a friendly atmosphere. Greatly responsible for this friendliness was the manager, a somewhat older man who had run his own similar business before the war.

Tom Bridges would sit with the staff during the lunch breaks. More and more he chose to sit beside Thea. He learned about Charlie and me; he told her his wife had died when both of them were still quite young.

She liked him, and when he eventually asked her out she agreed.
After several 'dates' she asked him home to meet the rest of her
family. My grandparents took to him, and apparently I did too. Tom,
Thea and I would go on outings throughout what was to be the last
eighteen months of the War.

***

My grandfather had a friend who was a senior officer in the Army
and he confirmed that there had been no recorded survivors from
the ship that Thea and my grandparents believed he was on. When,
a month after the surrender in August 1945, there had still been no
news of Charlie, my mother married Tom Bridges. She and I, now
two and a half years old, moved into his house.

***

Later that year the Americans occupying Japan received reports of
a group of Australian POWs at a mine site in the northern island of
Hokkaido. No mail had ever been passed on to them and none had
been permitted out; Charlie was there.

The Army offered to contact next-of-kin but Charlie asked to be
allowed to do it himself. With no brothers and sister, and with both
his parents dead, there was only one person he wanted to contact,
but he knew there was quite a possibility that she had a new
'friend', or had even married. He wrote to my grandfather, and he
wrote back with the news of Thea's marriage, begging him to leave
her in ignorance of his survival. She would be distraught, he said.
My grandfather made no mention of me.

When Charlie returned to Brisbane my grandparents went to see
him at the hospital. My grandmother was to tell me later that she
had to keep excusing herself from the ward, she was so upset.
"He was just skin and bone---and he'd been such a big healthy
man. I think I cried for weeks afterwards. But you know, he was
so understanding---noble really, that's the word. He promised he

103

wouldn't contact Thea---'just let her believe I died' he said. Fred offered him financial help and I know he did pay for a flat for him until he got back on his feet. He felt so badly for him---we both did. And oh, it was so hard not to say anything about you."

***

So Tom Bridges was my father during my early childhood---and I could not have had a better. Though he was quite old to have such a very young son---he would have been in his early fifties when he married my mother---he played backyard cricket with me and took me fishing and generally 'played' with me as a much younger dad might have done. He used to walk me to school when I was very young, and when I was older he came to the evening parents' nights with me.

When I was twelve years old however he and Thea decided I should be told about Charlie. They did it well, and I apparently *took* it well; *two* fathers, and one of them a war hero! I remember I felt it gave me extra status somehow.

About a year afterwards I plucked up the nerve to ask my mother to tell me more about Charlie, and how the two of them had met. She refused; she said that she loved Tom and we had a happy life and she didn't want to bring a ghost into it. Charlie was in the past and long gone, and we needed to leave him there.

I had a very close relationship with my mother; in a way it was more like that of contemporaries or equals than mother and son; like equals we indulged in fairly robust arguments at times, but I didn't argue that one about Charlie. I felt it was one occasion when I should just accept her wishes.

***

When I was sixteen Tom suddenly became ill, from a melanoma that had escaped detection, and he died within a few months. It was a horrible time for us; Tom had been a wonderful father to me and I think a wonderful husband to my mother.

It was a harder time for Thea than for me. I had all the activity of school and sport, and I had discovered the confusing but fascinating world of girls, so my life was full and exciting, but Thea, a stay-at-home mum, had more time and opportunity to grieve and regret. After a while she took a job at a local chemist's, as a sales assistant, and that I think helped a lot, taking her out of herself.

***

On my seventeenth birthday and during a visit to her parents' house I asked again, in front of all three of them, to be told more about my biological father. This time my mother agreed, but it was a difficult moment for the older couple. Their grandson was asking about his father, whom he believed to be dead, and they knew he had survived. They had still not told Thea, when they *could* have after Tom had died; they had come to the conclusion that it was best if she didn't know. (When I reminded them of that evening years later they said it had been excrutiating.)

Back at our own home that night my mother recounted the history of the very short courtship, and brought out the photos she had kept. The photos were all Brisbane CBD shots---Thea said that at that time there were many men taking commercial photos in the streets, and doing good business because of the soldiers.

I stared at the images. My parents looked so *young;* my mother could have been one of the girls in my class at high school. Charlie was in army uniform in each photo, but it was easy to see the *country man* there. He was tall, taller than I thought he'd be, and with quite a thick head of very blond hair. He was laughing, or so it seemed, in every shot---a tall, athletic, happy-go-lucky country boy. It was a surprise---I had somehow conceived more of an image of 'soldierliness'.

In every shot Charlie and Thea looked so happy. I was strongly moved by the photos; "never throw any of these away" I ordered.

***

I finished school and went to University, doing Law. During this time my mother's health began to fail, and she was eventually diagnosed with lung cancer. I couldn't believe it---my lively, effervescent mother---seriously ill. She hung on for three years; "I want to see you graduate."

We lost Thea in 1964, when I was twenty-two and she herself was still quite young. She always made light of her illness---a'bold' girl to the end.

***

I now believed that Gran and Granpa were all the family I had, but with Thea gone they felt they were free to tell me my father had survived the war. It was a big shock of course, and I decided to try and find him. The Army had all the details---he was in fact living in the town of Ipswich, just a little to the west of Brisbane, *and with a wife.*

***

Pearl had married Charlie, in 1946, after she had nursed him at a repatriation hospital. When I phoned Charlie it was she who answered. She was abrupt. "He won't want to see you. Please don't ring again. He's not well." She hung up.

I had already seen how frail Charlie was. When I had found out where they lived I had driven to their street and parked near their cottage. I did that twice, and on the second occasion saw them come out and get into a taxi. Pearl stood tall and straight, looking strong, but he walked uncertainly, wearing dark glasses and leaning on her arm.

I waited another day and rang again. "I *must* see him Mrs.Wheeler. He is my *father*. You must understand." She didn't hang up as she had before, and I put extra determination into my voice. "I'd like to come tomorrow morning." She agreed.

I wondered on and off for the rest of that day about her acquiescence. Had it been brought about by the not-to-be-denied tone in my voice---or had she told Charlie and he had said I must come----or had she herself simply had a change of heart?

***

They were waiting on their front verandah, he sitting in a big cane chair and she standing beside him. He was wearing the dark glasses but was smiling, that wide soft smile I had come to know well from the photos. She did not smile.

Charlie took both my hands in his. "This is Pearl" he said, with a nod in her direction but she did not come forward, and in fact took a tiny step back. There was hostility on her face---it was an effort to return her gaze.

I realised that Charlie was blind; he couldn't see his son! It was a shocking disappointment. But we talked---and while we did his wife scarcely looked at me, and said nothing; I was at a loss to understand her antagonism.

After an hour I wilted, driven away by her grim face. But Charlie had invited me to return soon and we arranged it for one week ahead. Pearl had still said not a word to me.

***

The second meeting was also on that verandah. It was winter---a windy day---but she did not suggest we move inside. When, after half an hour, she went to the kitchen to make tea Charlie told me she had tried to persuade him to cancel the meeting.

107

"Pearl's worried. We haven't managed to have kids and now you pop up and---well---I suppose she is a bit---I don't know, what would you say---well, unhappy anyhow. But oh", and here he reached over and found my shoulder and squeezed it, "I'm so glad you did son." I wept then---and she came out the front door and saw.

As I was leaving, Charlie stood and put out his arms out and I moved into them. As we hugged I looked over my father's shoulder at her. The hostility was still there, but then I saw the stiffness go from her shoulders. Her arms, which had been by her side, lifted slowly, as if of their own volition, and her hands came together over her breast. The coldness went from her eyes.

She came forward and put her arms around her husband's broad back, then moved closer until her hands rested on me too. The three of us stood together---one of the most wonderful moments of my life.

***

The poor diet in Japan, and the lack of medical care, had left Charlie's kidneys in a bad way. They were beginning to fail, and he was becoming weaker. I spent as much time as I could at their house, often taking him on the trips to the hospital. We became close, a closeness encouraged no doubt by intimations of mortality.

Charlie had only kind words to say about Thea, not judging her harshly for not having waited for him. He wanted to hear all about our lives---my own and Thea's, and Tom's too.

I wondered how much I should tell him---was it fair to Pearl? But the man really wanted to know, and I soon saw that *she* believed there was no harm in it. She was devoted to her husband, but I think she had decided that he---they---had nothing to fear from me. I realised I could say anything---I could *ask* anything; they made me feel that I could come to their home as often as I liked and stay as long as I liked. I was allowed to step right into their lives.

Pearl was splendid really; if she ever were jealous, because Charlie asked *me* to take him to the Mater, or on a drive in the car, or to sit alone with him on the verandah---sometimes for hours---she never showed anything like that, and I admired her greatly for it. I had found in her a new friend---and that beneath a calm and slightly forbidding exterior was a warm and affectionate nature.

***

At my father's funeral service she and I sat together. There were just a handful of other people, friends but no family. Back at the house we toasted Charlie, and his friends reminisced. Two men from the prisoner-of-war camp days told how Charlie had been their strength when things had been at their worst.

After the others had gone Pearl and I sat side by side on that verandah into the evening, I in Charlie's big cane chair.

***

We became mother and son, and I visited her often, and when I couldn't, I phoned. Very soon after beginning to go out with Patricia I took her over to meet Pearl, and after we were married Pat found in Pearl the perfect mother-in-law, as in time our daughters found in her the perfect grandmother.

Pearl's visits to our home were highlights of the girls' lives. If I were home early from my office they would insist that we all walk to the train station to meet her, and if she were not staying overnight--- and how the girls begged her to---we would all walk her back to the station after dinner.

When the girls were old enough they went on their own by train to Ipswich and stayed with her overnight. Patricia or I would ring, to find out how she was handling them, and more often that not we could hear them giggling and laughing up in her bedroom, where they were dressing up in her furs and high heels, and putting on her make-up.

109

Pearl was welcome in all our family activities---birthdays, christenings, Christmas, picnics, graduations---everything. As she grew older Pat and I tried to persuade her to come and live with us, but she said that while she loved visiting us she also loved going back to her home in the evening---the one she had bought with Charlie so long before.

***

At ninety two years of age Pearl finally acknowledged that she could no longer look after herself in that house, and she moved into a retirement home near us in Brisbane.

"I'm in a Home again---where I started off"---but this time she had many visitors. The director told me that they had never had a resident who received so many---and so many young ones---*great* grandchildren by now.

***

Last week Pearl became a great-great grandmother, and two days later she died. It was a peaceful passing, Pat and I with her at the end. Her eyes closed, she said softly "family", squeezed my hand--- and was gone.

ELEVEN

SOMETHING WHITE

He didn't know why she had asked him to let the damn things out---or why *he* had to put them back in again. It was not as if he came back to the place often now---and even when he did it wasn't because he wanted to; he was only here now to get a bit more of his gear. This time though there'd been the note about the leak in the house tank. He'd been inclined to leave it for her to fix because he knew it would take a couple of hours---emptying the thing first and then getting the pump going to fill it again; he wanted to be gone before she got back.

At least the birds were getting a good peck around---but god they were stupid, more stupid than chooks, and that was saying something. Why she had to go and get turkeys---but that was typical---always thought she knew best. And why *white* ones......?

The tank was nearly full now so he sent old Max around the birds to round them up; he was the only one of his three dogs he could trust not to try and eat the things. At least they were coming in quickly, that was one thing.

It would've been nice to see the girls, but no---he couldn't stand another argument with her---and that's how it would end up---

always did; they'd had nothing civil to say to each other for a long time. His mates told him it was because he'd married the wrong one, and he thought they were right. Should have married someone like Kev's Maureen---nice girl---never any dramas......

The birds were streaming back through the gate. He should take a couple---she wouldn't miss them. He could do a big cook up back at the mine---be good, all his mates....

A large black form shot past him.

***

The girls were arguing in the back seat but she said nothing. They were still a bit 'up' from their time at the pool with the other kids. They'd go to sleep soon.

Though she was always tired after the two days of teaching in town it was a satisfying kind of tiredness. She'd been glad to stop teaching when she got married and they had moved out onto the property, but now she found she was enjoying it again. She believed she was doing it better now too---perhaps having her own kids had helped there---and the money was so useful now.

She liked the hour's drive home on the Friday afternoons---and for the past three months there'd been the extra pleasure of seeing again her three hundred white-feathered babies.

The turkeys had been her own idea and really they hadn't been much trouble. She wasn't sure what the neighbours thought but she didn't care. She had been able to forward sell almost all the birds in town. The money was going to mean at least a decent Christmas, and possibly a holiday.

Roberta and Suzie loved the birds and watched over them better than she did, especially when she let them out in the afternoon to scratch around the homestead. It was the girls who found the dead one in the second week, and who told her if any were "a bit sick." Which had been very few; after three months there had been only four casualties. The Department man said he'd never seen such a healthy flock.

John hated them---seemed to hate the *idea* of them. Maybe hated *her* a bit more too because of them. Well, all that was coming to a head---had to.

***

His mind was racing now, thinking of everything. Everything and nothing. He knew one thing---he would never go back---could never go back. He drove fast, the dogs locked once again in their mesh cage on the back of the ute.

He didn't know how the young dog had got out. It didn't matter anyhow because who'd believe he hadn't set it free deliberately? He had tried to call the animal back but had seen it kill one bird then another and then something wicked had risen in him and he had gone to the ute and let the other one go.

He didn't know how many they must have killed---even old Max had joined in; the dogs had only come back to him when they were exhausted. He had loaded them again, turned off the pump and driven away.

***

She woke the girls when there was about a kilometre to go, at the spot where the home ridge came into sight. One said, almost immediately, "look Mum," and pointed ahead: something white, on the road.

TWELVE

LIKE ERROL

I own a few businesses in this town including a motel---my town's budget one. "Clean, Comfortable, Affordable" is our creed---or more correctly that of Errol, my manager.

I drop in there about once a week to talk things over with Errol. He's easy to find---I just have to switch the engine off and listen. If he's not talking with someone, joking and laughing---and he does have a carrying voice---he's *singing*. He favours the rock numbers of the 60's---Elvis, Bobby Darin, the Everly Brothers---all those.

I don't know what the customers think of him---although I suppose I do because they *keep returning*. I sometimes read the filled-in 'Invitation to Comment' forms the girls leave in the rooms. If there is a witty remark about his style---or his singing---he puts it up on the office wall. That's like Errol.

***

This is a medium size town in the mid-west of Queensland. My oldest business here is an agency, selling fertilizer and drenches and implements and machinery---anything and everything for farms. Five years ago Errol walked into the agency and asked me for a job.

He told me he'd grown up on a dairy on the coast, worked at the local milk factory and then moved up to Rockhampton with his wife and got a job in a big hardware and farm supplies store. As he described it, his job there involved a bit of everything but mainly serving customers.

I know the store; it is huge, and looks a bit old-fashioned, but over the years it has built up a very good reputation, particularly for service. I happen to know through a business contact that its turnover is enormous.

I hadn't remembered seeing this solidly-built, energetic looking young man the last time I called there but now as he talked I could imagine him on the job there---racing around the counters, serving two customers at once and assuring another he would be just a minute---that sort of person. He told me he liked it there but it was a wage job with not enough incentive and he was looking for something more. He said he had always been interested in moving out west and, flatteringly, told me he had heard I ran a good business.

My profit depends on sales, and as it happened I *had* been thinking of putting on another salesman. Errol said if I took him on he would like to be paid on a straight commission basis---a mark I thought of his self-confidence. When I said that I would consider him I got a big grin and another vigorous handshake. He'd come prepared, and gave me the names and phone numbers of two people as references; I always use my own sources though to check out possible employees, and within a day I had learned all I needed.

Because I know that it can be hard for a newcomer if he is depending only on commissions I offered him a base salary as well---the same deal as my other employees had; within a fortnight Errol was up and running.

***

I did wonder if I might have got hold of a tiger by the tail. An agricultural agency such as mine depends as much on personal relations and reputation as it does upon prices. A *regular* client will buy from us even if he can get whatever it is a bit cheaper somewhere else---and if we don't have what he wants he knows we will get it in for him. If he returns something that he says is faulty he can rely on us to replace it or have it repaired. If he cannot pay for a few months he knows we will accommodate him.

What I was edgy about with Errol was that he might put 'the deal' above all else, just to earn that commission. I could imagine him guaranteeing delivery of something when we couldn't, or talking someone into buying something he really didn't need, or couldn't afford. I took pains to get across to him that the *people* side of the business was the most important.

Well, I needn't have worried. He did increase our turnover---considerably---but for all his 'go' he was a people person too; I think people found that purchasing something through friendly Errol was just the natural end to a meeting with him.

There were times when he came back from visiting a farmer with an order so much bigger than we had ever had from that person that I felt sure we'd get a phone call changing it---but it didn't happen. Errol untied some of the district's tightest purse strings, and seemingly without effort.

His phone technique was a revelation. His calls sounded simply social---no hint of a 'sell'. Somehow it was the client himself who came up with the idea of buying something---or thought he did.

At a Field Day or the annual Show where we had our own tent and a display of machinery and implements he was unstoppable. He would make sure we had tables and folding chairs and sandwiches and tea and cold drinks, and once again what had all the appearance of a social get together delivered a lot of business.

***

You can imagine it was with mixed feelings I learned that after just two years with me he wanted to leave the agency and run the motel I had just purchased. "But you're doing so well here!" I said. And so, as a consequence, was I. "You're earning twice as much as you were on the coast."

"I know but I'll be good for the motel. And you can find someone to do this. I'll help you find him."

"You like this job Errol. Let me find another Errol to run the motel."

"I've thought about it; it's what I'd really like to do." My face must have been a study because he said "I'll start off on an ordinary wage," but then, because this was Errol, " when I build it up though I'd like to share in that. More like partners."

Smiling---and so keen what could one do.

***

It turned out that Errol was perfect for the Sunset. It took on a different look and atmosphere from the day he went there. He painted all the timberwork and made the entrance more attractive and renewed the lawns and put in more shrubs and trees. He put up a new sign and had "Under New Management" put on a board underneath. The place got a lot busier; we didn't increase our rates but the returns jumped.

He wanted to put our prices on a sandwich board at the driveway entrance but I was against that. I had always felt that if I saw such a sign outside a motel it was an indication that it wasn't doing well. Another thing was that I didn't want to enter a price war with the other motel in town.

"It won't happen," said Errol. "Mrs Porter doesn't need to drop her prices. She shouldn't. It's a different clientele."

I argued my other point---about it making the place look a bit 'desperate'. Errol looked at me for a few seconds without saying anything, as if gathering his thoughts---unusual for him to do that.

"I do the opposite. I always look for that price board. I want to know before I drive in that I can afford it. I don't want to have to drive out again to go somewhere else."

It was a reminder to me of the difference in our financial situations, and how my wealth was cutting me off from the experiences of people like him. We did it his way.

***

Errol never collected his wife from Rockhampton. He said in the early days that he was waiting to get a suitable house. He would drive back each weekend---but then these trips became irregular. He began turning up at parties with local girls; he got the nickname 'Flynn' of course.

The only concern I have ever had with Errol is over his love life, about which he is very enthusiastic. In the two years he was at the agency he had a variety of 'friends', around town and in the district. It seemed that they couldn't say no to him and he couldn't say no to them.

Rural Queensland is a conservative place and I thought Errol's activities might have harmed our business, but it didn't seem to do that. Whatever magic he worked must have been strong because I never heard anything bad about him, even from the family or friends of a girl he had romanced and left behind.

Just after he settled in at Sunset he said he'd need an assistant manager because of the long work hours. He had a woman picked out, someone whom I did not know but who seemed the right type when I met her. I did wonder if she and Errol were lovers and it turned out to be so.

Eileen stayed for a year (a long time for Errol) then there was Lisa and now there's Sharon. They've all been competent and nice and, though the arrangement is irregular and wouldn't appear I am sure in any manual on 'best business practice', it seems to have worked. I suppose there are some people in town who disapprove but I take the view that it's harming no-one. There are far worse things happening around us I'm sure---and meanwhile business at the Sunset is booming.

*****

I like going to the motel; I go about nine in the morning. This is the busiest time of the day, with people checking out and staff beginning to clean the rooms---the worst time to try to talk with a manager you would think, especially a hands-on type like Errol Makim, and we do get a lot of interruptions.

I used to phone before coming to the motel but Errol kept telling me to come unannounced. Then I would pick a quiet time, like after lunch, but he didn't like that either; he told me---I remember his saying it---that if *he* owned a motel he'd want to see it when it was at its busiest. So I took his suggestion and I am glad I did; I get more idea of how things are going from fifteen hectic minutes than I would from an hour of quiet talk. I even get dragged into taking phone bookings and advising people on their trips, and enjoy it.

It's interesting too that although Errol's been managing the motel for three years he isn't looking for a break. He has holidays of course but what I mean is that he wants to *continue with the job*. I've talked with other motel owners and they say it's very hard to find someone who will stay year after year---and if they do stay on they tend to become irritable.

I've met managers like that when I've stayed somewhere. I used to think they were in the wrong job---and I do think it's a job that suits only some people. It wouldn't suit me; I am a people person to some extent I suppose but I like my solitude too and you don't seem to get enough of that when you run a motel. Anyway, now when I meet an owner or manager who is a bit 'short' I think he probably just needs a break. Not like Errol.

**

I do not know how good a 'boss' I am but I have had a lot of experience in business and have employed a lot of people. I tell new employees that it is not *I* who pays their wages but our customers. The good ones grasp this concept; I think Errol *was born knowing it*. I am so lucky he walked through my door five years ago.

**

Last week I was in Rockhampton when Errol rang me at my hotel. He was down in the city for the day too and would I meet him in the lounge for lunch and a drink? He wanted to introduce me to someone.

So I met his ex-wife---and we had a really nice time. She enjoyed the stories Errol and I told about life out west. When she left I got a hug but Errol got a bigger hug and a kiss. Seems we all like Errol.

THIRTEEN

FINDING GRACE

In 1950 I was sent as a very young primary school teacher to a town in the central west of Queensland---I shall call it "Hartwood"---close to the Tropic of Capricorn and some four hundred kilometres from the coast. In those days much of the road from the coast was unsealed and the trip by car or truck could take nearly two days---longer if there had been rain---but fortunately the town was on a rail line. In fact Hartwood was the railhead.

The land round about Hartwood was given over to the running of beef cattle, as I understand it still is. Although there was quite a community of people at each homestead in those days, the properties themselves were so huge that the country overall was only very lightly populated.

The town itself was not very big, but it was a busy place, and I think this was largely due to the railway. People today do not realise, I am sure, just how important the railway line once was to country life--- for jobs and business.

Because Hartwood *was* such a hub, people from a wide area sent their children there for schooling, boarding them at the government or church hostels, or with family or friends. My school had many more children than most other country towns of that size would have had; we had *six* primary school teachers.

 Our principal was a woman, Grace Metcalf, who, at the time I arrived, had already been at the school for five years. She was to become one of the most important people in my life.

***

Going to a small town far from family and friends can be a daunting thing for a young female teacher---and this was my first country posting---but my settling into Hartwood was made much easier by Grace Metcalf. For one thing, she sought my company, which was surprising to me because she seemed much older than I.

In time I would learn that she was in fact only thirty but she *presented* as older; she dressed in rather plain clothes, wore her hair back in a tight bun and used little or no make-up. Also, she was married---to the assistant station master, Ray Metcalf. They had no children.

In my first few weeks at Hartwood Grace frequently asked me to wait after classes to talk about some aspect of the schoolwork. I came to realise she *liked* talking to me---that she liked *me*---and that was marvellous. As we got to know each other the 'generation' difference melted away, and Grace and I became good friends.

***

I was boarding with a family in the town, very comfortably, but Grace would often invite me round to her house on weekends. Ray Metcalf was generally out at these times---at first I thought that he must have been at work but soon realised it was more likely to be a hotel. If he *were* at home he did not talk much to me and, I noticed, didn't talk much to Grace either.

The house was always spic and span. When I complimented Grace on this once she said that that was how Ray liked it. She

124

made splendid meals and something she said made me think that these also were for Ray's benefit---but I never heard any *thanks or acknowledgement* from him. I actually began to feel resentment on her behalf; this woman, who was so helpful to her fellow teachers, seemed to be unappreciated in her own home.

(A reader might be wondering where all this is leading. I'm a great reader of novels, even at this age, and I know that this is what is called 'scene setting'. I probably have quite a bit more of this to do, but I will pause here and say that there are three females who are important to this story and in Grace you have met the most important one. Actually they are all equally important, but she is the one I choose to begin with, and will end with. Three heroines in this one story---and one hero.)

***

 My second heroine is MaryTomasetti. She was nine years old when I arrived in town, tall for her age, healthy and strong. She had a mass of auburn hair, like her Italian mother, Sophia, but with more aquiline features. Attractive though, with a particularly direct and intelligent gaze.

She was not in one of my classes but I certainly knew who she was. Her name often came up in our staff room because she was such a favourite. She had a thirst for knowledge and a phenomenal memory; she was the kind of child that makes a teacher's job a pleasure. She was also however the victim of gossip because, you see, her mother was unmarried.

***

Sophia, her mother---and my third 'heroine'---worked at Carmody's, the biggest hotel in the town. I was told that she had simply arrived in town on the mail truck one day and Carmody had immediately given her a job. She began as one of the bar maids but progressed quickly to managing all the bars then the dining room as well and then, it seemed, the whole place. A dozen or so years after arriving seemingly penniless she was running what was a very big business, and assumed to be very well paid.

However, three years after she arrived, Sophia became pregnant. It created a scandal of course, made all the more intriguing because she did not talk of any marriage plans and did not tell anyone who the father was. People assumed it was Carmody but he did not say anything either.

By the time the child was three years old the question of paternity had been settled to everyone's satisfaction because the girl quite clearly had inherited some of Carmody's facial features. Her parents though still made no move to marry, and this was in a way even more of a scandal, because so far as the town knew there was no impediment.

The accepted belief was that it was Ted Carmody, the life long bachelor---he must have been nearly sixty by then---who would not front the altar. The women of the town were divided in their feelings over this. Many vilified him---were incensed that he would not 'do the right thing.' Others blamed Sophia; they said that an attractive woman like her---and she was *very* attractive---could *make* him marry, and that she was not trying.

I was surprised at the strength of feeling some people still exhibited---and the girl by now nine years old! One woman that I overheard at a fete spoke quite viciously.

"Was that Kath McCartney?" Grace asked when I mentioned it to her.

"As a matter of fact it was."

"Ray tells me her Fred makes quite a fool of himself over Sophia at the pub."

***

One lunchtime I happened to be in Grace's office when young Mary came to the door, her clothes rumpled and her hair a tangle. She said she had been sent by Miss Bott for fighting. Grace did not ask the reason for the fight; lately some girls had taken to taunting Mary and calling her and her mother names, and there had been two fights already.

Grace beckoned the girl inside and, taking a brush from somewhere, cleaned the dust off her clothes. With another brush she tidied her hair. "Try to ignore those girls Mary," she said as she sent her off, and then to me, "this has to stop, Ruth."

"Will you call those other girls in?"

"I have done that---twice. It's coming from their parents of course. Their mothers. I will have to do something else."

**

One afternoon, having just sent my children home for the day, I was standing on the verandah when one of our cleaners came up.

Belle did her part-time work with great vigour; I used to wonder how it was that a woman in her sixties could bring such dedication to a menial job like cleaning. I liked her, and she always seemed to find time for a chat with me.

As she put down her broom and bucket we looked out across the playground just as Mary came out of her classroom and began to walk towards the gate. I watched her, with no particular thought in mind, and Belle watched her too.

"She's a love."

"Yes," I said, "but I wish….. "

"I know," said Belle, "but nothing's going to happen there."

"If Mr Carmody would just marry her mother….."

"He won't, love," she said, and then she told me what she knew about him.

***

Ted Carmody had been brought up in Charters Towers. His parents had gone there like many others because of the gold, but instead of prospecting they had established a store. They prospered, and eventually retired to the coast. When they died they left five thousand pounds each to their son and their two daughters. Ted was about thirty-five then.

"He wasn't married," said Belle. "He'd worked on the mines and on boats. A man's world, love---no women. Nice women, if you know what I mean. Plenty of the other sort."

Ted hadn't spent his inheritance. "Didn't bank it either. Took it with him wherever he went, he told me."

He continued a wandering life but apparently had decided he wanted a hotel. When he came to Hartwood the town's largest and oldest hotel was on the market and he bought it.

***

He adopted the habit of working full time at the hotel for eleven months of the year then putting on a manager for a month and taking himself south for a holiday---by train, to Sydney or Melbourne. One year he took a coastal steamer from Melbourne to Perth.

"He'd set himself up in a big city hotel and splash his money around and pretty soon a good looking girl would turn up. Two or three weeks of 'married life' and then he'd come back to the bush. He's a natural bachelor love."

Belle picked up her things and bustled to the door of my classroom. "If you ask me, a lot of men out here are like Ted Carmody."

A week later, Grace told me she had been to see the girl's mother.

"Where?"

"At the hotel. I sent a note with Mary and Sophia sent one back. Carmody was away and she said she couldn't leave the hotel but she asked me to go there."

She showed me a sheet with a 'Carmody Hotel' letterhead. The last line read "Mary talks about you quite a lot. You are one of her favourite people."

"Disarming...."

"Wasn't it. Anyhow I went down there. The front door was locked for some reason and I had to go in through the main bar. Do you know, that was the first time I had ever been in a public bar. Have you?"

I shook my head. Women did not go into bars in those days; I am not sure if it was actually legal. "What was it like?"

"Dark and quiet. Hardly any chairs. There were a few men standing over at the bar. I didn't look at them; I didn't particularly want to be recognised! I went through another door into the main foyer. One of the staff must have got word to Sophia because she met me there. Very pleasant, very welcoming."

"What did you say?"

"Well straight off *she* said she supposed this was about the fighting and I said yes. We went back to her office and she said this had happened before and asked me how I thought it was affecting her daughter. I said ---as you and I have noticed---not much at all, but that she was a remarkable child.

She agreed and said she had spent some time explaining to the girl that this kind of thing would happen but how, in the long run, it was unimportant. And then she asked if I would have a sherry with her and you know what, I said yes. Dutch courage. Then she said straight out that her staying single should be of no business to anyone else."

"That was telling you!"

"But she didn't say it offensively. It did make me question what on earth I had thought I would say to the woman. "Please fix this situation and marry the man?"

"What *did* you say?"

"Well---this is bizarre---I started talking about myself!"

"Why?"

"I don't know. Nervousness possibly. I started to tell her about what it was like to run a school and about the rewards and all that and she listened and asked some good questions. She is a smart woman Ruth. And she has a real presence you know. Anyhow, I chattered on like a child. And when a girl brought in a second sherry---I took it."

I was amazed. I had never seen Grace drink anything alcoholic. "*Two* fallen women."

"Yes," Grace laughed. "Isn't it funny. Anyhow Sophia, when she *was* able to get a word in, talked about *her* job. And every now and then one of the staff came in to ask or tell her something. You know, that big business was being run from that desk by that woman while we were talking---and with all female staff. It was---inspiring. I knew a couple of the women too. Holly Fisher---doesn't she have a girl in your class? I am afraid my visit will be all over town by now."

"But what did you......? "

"What did I achieve? Nothing I suppose. Except I learned one thing. It is not Ted who won't marry *her*. It's the other way around. Isn't that something?"

"Doesn't she---love him?"

"I can't believe it now but that's what I asked her. It must have been the sherry. She didn't seem to mind; she said 'as much as I am ever likely to love anybody.' But she said she wanted to stay single *and independent.* She said she had grown up in a family that expected her to marry the boy they had picked out for her. She didn't want to be like the other Italian women she knew; she saw them as mere child bearers and slaves. Bossed by men. She said she rejected that at nineteen and she was still rejecting it."

"What did you say?"

"Well it was powerful stuff but I said I thought Ted wouldn't be like that. She agreed, but said she believed he accepted her the way she was. She said that they were a family already---just a different kind."

***

I thought about what Grace had told me quite a lot over the next few days. Young women today probably cannot imagine how radical Sophia's view was. Back then, women were identified by their marriage, to a great extent. A woman was *Mrs. So and So.* If 'So and So' was successful or prominent or rich then so was his wife. Clever girls made sure they married 'well'---which meant marrying someone who would provide security. But even marrying *anyone* was thought to be preferable to not being married at all.

You must remember too that there were very few good paying jobs for women then. And there was certainly no government support for a single mother.

And the final extraordinary thing was that Sophia was *Italian.* You'd have to say that meant *conservative.* Traditional. Her stand was as unlikely back then as, say, having a person of Chinese background becoming Prime Minister.

However, the woman was in a very secure position financially. She was probably earning a lot more than Grace---probably more than most of the men in the town. She had a large apartment in the hotel and, we guessed, would receive a significant amount of money from Ted Carmody's estate, come the time.

"Yes, that is all very well for Sophia," said Grace when we talked again a few days later, "and I actually think she is a good mother all round. But it's hard on that little girl, don't you think?"

I did---although there had been no more name calling or fighting for several weeks. Perhaps, I thought---or hoped---that would just fade away. But then her teacher intercepted a note that was being passed from child to child in the classroom; "Mary is a bastard."

"I have to stop this," Grace said that afternoon.

***

The next day was a Saturday and as usual I did some shopping in the main street. I saw Grace talking with Ted Carmody on the footpath and later, when I went into the café for a drink, I saw them again. They were at a table at the rear and I waved when Grace caught my eye but did not move to join them---there was a set to Grace's shoulders and neck that I recognised; she was 'on the case' as people say today.

Carmody looked calm---uninterested almost---as he always did. Do you remember the actor Robert Mitchum? Carmody had that same sleepy look. But he *was* listening, occasionally saying something; I watched now and then, out of the corner of my eye---discreetly I thought.

***

"You were spying on us," Grace said on the Monday, but smiling.

"You were up to something."

"And oh Ruth, I may have succeeded."

"What? Tell me."

She paused, "I can't. I really can't say anything just yet. Sorry. I am hoping though we will hear something very soon."

And three days later we did and, from all sources, young Mary. It was during her class's "Today's News" period, an initiative Grace had introduced to get the kiddies to take an interest in local events and to be able to talk about them. It was a favourite of the teachers, but we never knew what we would hear. Sometimes it was something quite private which a family would hate to have spread around. We had to be on our toes.

This day Mary Tomasetti told her class that she was to be *adopted* by Ted and she would change her name to Carmody. "Mummy will still be my mummy but Mr Carmody will be my daddy." Then the child added, "I won't be a bastard anymore." Can you imagine!

"What did you do?" we asked her teacher.

"When I gathered my wits I said that this was wonderful news and I thought we should be very happy for Mary. The Paulsen twins, who play a lot with Mary, ran over and hugged her. You should have seen Mary's face. She was just beaming."

***

"So that's what you were talking about in the café?"

"Yes."

"It was your idea, wasn't it?"

"Oh---you know you shouldn't ask me that."

But I kept looking at her and she nodded. "I thought, just because Sophia won't marry Ted that shouldn't be the end of the matter and then this came to me. It's so neat because Ted is her father anyhow."

"What was his reaction?"

"Not marked---at the time. Well, he doesn't show much reaction to anything does he? Not his style. I just kept talking and he just went on buttering those pikelets they serve. When I asked him what he thought he just nodded. I asked him how he thought Sophia would react, and he nodded again. Never stopped eating. I thought 'well, I've done what I can.'

You know, I had screwed myself up so tight to have that meeting that on my walk back home I was shaking."

"But happy."

"But happy."

"And triumphant."

"Ruth no," she smiled "but yes, a little bit proud of myself."

"Well, you've done the right thing by the child."

Grace frowned. "Sophia Tomasetti is a good woman and a good mother. She has an exceptional child and she is rearing her well. Sophia is not like you or me or most women."

***

The next edition of the "Hartwood Gazette" carried a Public Notice and there was an interview by the editor of Sophia and Ted. They said they had consulted a solicitor and he was submitting forms to various Government departments. They hoped the community would support them and young Mary.

It certainly gave 'the community' something to talk about but the talk went on very quietly. People seemed to understand that Ted and Sophia were doing this to make life easier for young Mary.

***

Ted Carmody took to walking Mary the five blocks to school. It was quite the novelty to see that big man and the little girl together, Mary walking slightly in front; the pair reminded me of a little tug leading a ship into harbour. Sophia would come in the afternoons and walk the girl home.

The walking of children to and from school in that town at that time was unusual. Even the littlies came and went on their own. I think Ted and Sophia did it to reinforce the new family status---to help Mary---and there was no more unpleasantness.

Ted also took to coming to the school whenever there was something on, like a sports meeting or a concert. Then he began to come to parents' meetings and to raise things he felt the school needed, like more shade areas in the playground, and musical instruments.

He had always responded before this to requests for funds to improve the school but now he took the lead. If Ted raised a need at a meeting it meant he would put up the money straightaway. Of course the group soon elected him President, and our school was rewarded with a stream of money and facilities. I recall one occasion when a train trip to the coast was mooted. We knew that many of the parents would not be able to afford to allow their child to go but 'an anonymous donor' offered to cover all costs. Ted's adoption of his daughter proved to be a boon to both Mary and the whole school.

***

My reserved head mistress and the more extroverted hotel manager found they enjoyed each other's company. Because Sophia was rarely free to leave the hotel, especially if Ted Carmody were away, Grace took to going down there. Sophia had a private section of the first floor verandah opening off her apartment, and the two would sit out there on warm evenings. I was asked to join them on occasion.

It was interesting to observe the change in Grace at those times: more relaxed, even in her posture. She laughed at Sophia's stories---and Sophia had seen enough to provide endless material. In her different sphere a teacher also sees and hears a lot, and a headmistress more so. Grace told stories too, ones I had not heard---more 'colourful' ones shall we say. She would take a drink with Sophia, and I did too. Just one, or perhaps two.

(I enjoyed those nights---they felt like parties. Today's young teachers would laugh at that but I was a young single female school teacher in a small town in mid-western Queensland and it was sixty years ago---a conservative world).

One night, after Grace or I had admired a dress Sophia was wearing (and she always wore expensive, beautifully made clothes) she fetched another dress, silk, dark blue and just lovely. It would have cost me a whole fortnight's salary.

"You could wear this Grace."

Grace demurred but Sophia made her go inside and put it on. The women were of the same height but Sophia had the fuller figure. She pinned any loose material behind Grace and we stepped back to inspect. It *did* suit Grace, but Sophia said 'more make-up'. Grace protested, but Sophia went to work with lipstick and eye shadow; the result was quite spectacular. The sensibly dressed teacher changed into a glamorous sophisticate.

Sophia brought out more dresses and outfits and Grace and I tried them all. There were two full-length cheval mirrors in the apartment and we posed and preened between them, and catwalked up and down. We had a real fashion show for several hours and it was great fun.

Men would dismiss that sort of thing I am sure as frivolous and of course it was---we were like school girls---but I believe that there is a place for that sort of frivolity in our lives. We can let our guard down and let real feelings come out.

Men could learn from 'women's business'. I have overheard enough conversations between men in staffrooms and at social functions to believe they are not good at getting to know each other. Not really getting to know.

I certainly learned a lot about Sophia on those evenings and one big thing I realised was that her being of Italian blood scarcely meant anything. Not that Sophia had become Anglo Saxon---she was just 'Australian': a smart, capable, confident, relaxed---and funny---Australian.

***

Sometimes Sophia would manage to get away from the hotel for a few hours on the weekend and come up to Grace's house, and it was there about three months after the adoption announcement that I first saw Grace assert herself with her husband Ray.

It was a late Sunday afternoon and there were four of us, we three and Hetty Brown, one of Sophia's staff who was the mother of one of our school children. We were sitting in the back yard and Ray was inside the house somewhere.

Ray did not join us whenever we met there. If it was a cool day we used the kitchen and Ray stayed in the lounge room, listening to the wireless or reading. On warm days we used the front verandah or, like this, sat under the Poinciana behind the house.

It wasn't unusual back then for a man not to mix with his wife's female friends. If they called at his house he might greet them and chat a bit but soon go off to some other part of the dwelling, or out to his shed. At parties and dances the men congregated at one end, the women at the other, and as I have said, hotel bars were for men only.

Young men and women mix together so much more easily these days don't they. When I pass a beer garden or an outdoor café I think it's marvellous to see all the young ones together.

In any case though, Ray Metcalf was a taciturn individual. It was hard to imagine his being very communicative even with a group of men at a pub. (At Grace's he wouldn't have got a word in anyhow. You know what it's like if four women get together---at least three of us are talking at once).

Anyhow, on this day---at about four o'clock---Ray came to the back door and asked "are we going to have a cup of tea?" Instead of excusing herself and going inside as she normally would have done, Grace said "I was just thinking of it dear. Will you get it going? There's fruit cake in a tin on the dresser." And when he called out a few minutes later that the kettle was boiling she replied "go ahead and make it Ray. A big pot."

This seems such a little thing, thinking of it now, but that was the first time I had seen Grace ask her husband to do any domestic thing. I must have had a funny look on my face because Sophia caught my eye and raised her eyebrows.

***

Like a good headmistress, Grace supported her staff, protecting us against ignorant or bullying bureaucrats in Brisbane and shielding us from the worst of the local parents. In our work she encouraged and challenged us, and any criticisms she offered of our performances were constructive and carefully given; she was friendly, but always 'the headmistress'.

Now we observed changes in her; she began to bring a lighter touch to her own work, not treating every problem as seriously as she had before. She spent more time in the staff room and less in her own office.

Her appearance changed too. She began to wear brighter clothes , and to use more colourful accessories. She had her hair cut short in a bob, and began to use more make-up. The change was gradual but marked. People use the term 'make over' these days and that was what it was. I thought it was wonderful.

***

In mid December Grace decided to hold a Christmas social for the teachers and any parents who wanted to come. It was meant to last just an hour or two, where people would chat and have a drink or two and then go home to dinner---like what one would call a cocktail party---but it developed into much more than that.

Two of the three members of the "Blue Rose" were parents of children at the school and they offered to come along and play background music. Carmody offered to provide the drinks and several of the mothers said they would bring food.

We thought that probably only twenty or thirty people would turn up so we decided to use the staff room instead of the hall. We stacked our desks on the verandah and put up some Christmas decorations.

Possibly because some anticipation was building about our little party we women decided to dress up a bit. I wore a nice ankle length cream lace dress with a wide emerald green sash. Grace chose a black dress with red earrings and red clips in her hair.

Well, three times as many people as we expected turned up---and the mood became festive. After a while the band members forgot their intention to play 'background' and increased the volume. They also began to play real dance music, quicksteps and foxtrots. A couple started dancing and soon the floor in the centre of the room was crowded.

The band played a waltz and Ted and Sophia began to step out; Ted was wearing his usual blue suit but Sophia was in a multi-coloured full skirted silk dress, a real bird of paradise. They danced well and looked good, and others stopped and left the floor to watch. Eventually they had the floor to themselves and when the waltz finished we clapped. Sophia laughed and curtseyed and Ted---big unresponsive Ted---bowed. Grace walked over to them;

as they stood together I thought what a good sight it was---and an appropriate one for us and the school and that year.

***

A fortnight later I left for Brisbane for the Christmas holidays. My mother was unwell, and because I was her only unmarried daughter I decided I should stay there. I got a position at a suburban school--- but I was very sorry to leave Hartwood.

Grace stayed on there, and we wrote to each other often. After three years she accepted a headmistress position at a big school in Brisbane and so we used to meet up again. Ray did not come to Brisbane as he and Grace had gone their separate ways. Grace told me it was she who had made the decision. "We were unsuited to each other Ruth. You would have seen that."

I married a teacher and we moved up to Cairns. Ray agreed to divorce Grace and she took her maiden name again. When she was in her fifties she took a long trip through the south and decided to live in Melbourne.

She retired as a full time teacher many years ago but she has continued to tutor from home---mainly children who are having difficulties in literacy. She is in her nineties but still does it. We still write; she never re-married.

I kept in touch with Sophia too---a letter perhaps once a year; she died about ten years ago. She inherited the hotel from Ted and in turn she left it to her daughter. Mary runs the hotel herself and I understand has become a very wealthy businesswoman. She has not married.

***

My husband and I are in our eighties now but still very healthy ; we are planning to visit Grace in Melbourne this year. I am so looking forward to that---we will have so much to talk about.

I do wonder what Grace makes of her life---as I wonder sometimes about my own. She has served others all of hers---helping children learn---helping them find themselves. I think though that during that year we shared in the little town in Queensland she also learned to find herself.

FOURTEEN

NEW PEOPLE

I had never been a super-fit guy---never played any sport at a top level---but I have always tried to keep active. When I reached forty I thought I should join a gym---and there are several in my town---but as I used to be a reasonable tennis player I inquired first at some courts near my home; did they have a social club that played regularly and which might be open to an extra member?

The answers were yes and yes; there was a group that had two courts booked two nights each week and as it happened had lost two of their regulars recently and would welcome a newbie. The manager of the courts said that the standard was fairly high. I 'tried out' one night and have been playing with the group there now for five years.

***

I teach English and History at one of the two high schools in this town, which is a fairly big one several hours drive north of Brisbane. At some time I made the mistake of admitting to the Department that I had majored in Psychology so I was also made Counsellor for both schools.

Dealing with 'troubled' kids and their sometimes even more troubled parents is now the most stressing part of my job; I have found that the regular tennis games, while helping to keep the body in some sort of shape, have also helped my mind: therapy if you like.

There are twenty members in the club but we generally get only sixteen or so turn up on any one night; the age range is from early twenties to about fifty. I am the only teacher, the rest are tradesmen---carpenters, plumbers, mechanics---and there are a couple of office workers, one of these our only female member. We rarely get anyone new; the last one was a builder who moved here from Brisbane just over a year ago---and that was when things began to change.

***

I go fairly full-on during a game and don't engage in much conversation then. For me, talk-time is when we are in the clubhouse between games, or beforehand, when a few early birds gather. A funny thing though is that, up to a year or so ago, little in the way of what I would call *conversation* took place.

As you can imagine, because of my training and profession I notice speech and behaviour patterns, and what stood out in our group was that when one or the other did say something *it was not followed up*. Mostly the 'something' was an opinion or a statement, generally delivered emphatically, and generally about sport or current political shenanigans. The opinion or statement might prompt another opinion or statement---usually to the contrary---but *no discussion*.

My wife attends an all-female class at a gym, and apparently there is almost non-stop chat there, before and during the action. I once told her about how stilted the communication was amongst our group; it pleased her to refer to us from then on as 'Early Man'. "Don't forget your club" was one of her regular witticisms as I left.

However---early last year---while I was out on the court one night and up on the net in a doubles game---I heard Frank in the clubhouse deliver one of his opinions in his fairly loud voice and then heard another voice, quieter and in *a questioning tone*. Unusual. Frank then *added a little more*. Unprecedented. A couple of the other men then said things, again in raised tones, and then the same low voice said something---still too quietly for me to hear what---and things steadied down again.

Several evenings later the same phenomenon occurred again but this time I happened to be sitting off. An utterance of Gerry's about asylum seekers, given in his usual not-to be-questioned tone, *was* questioned by Tony, the new man---the builder from Brisbane. A couple of other men stated their positions---in *their* usual manner--- but Tony argued, and well I thought, not putting their views down but 'opening up' the subject. An interesting discussion followed; I joined in.

I was surprised---impressed---and after I went home berated myself a little. With my training and experience *I* could have done this sort of thing; why had I not? I told myself it was because, when I was there, I was *off duty*---but I know the main reason was that I had thought it would scarcely be worthwhile; I had lumped most of my fellow club members in a category and been content to leave them there. Full marks to the new man, I thought.

***

One coolish night soon after this, while I was warming up on one of the exercise bikes they have in the clubhouse, Tony climbed onto another bike beside me.

"Good idea" he said.

I quizzed him; I learned that he had been an independent builder in Brisbane, doing mainly private homes. He had married and had two children but was now divorced. He had prime custody of his children and they were now attending the 'other' high school here. I did not know of them, which, I can say as Counsellor, was a definite point in their favour.

The man was an easy talker, with an open manner. He told me he had always wanted to live in a country town and was very happy with the one he had chosen.

***

In the weeks that followed Tony and I exchanged greetings but did not manage another real conversation. He did have conversations with some of the others though, often while he was playing. Sometimes he brought along a book for someone.

He came across to me as a balanced individual, happy with himself and very interested in other people. Popular: whenever he turned up one or more of the others always walked over to him. And--- some people have it all don't they---he was physically attractive: wide shouldered, lean, fit and tall---Sean Conneryish. He looked about my age.

***

One evening, when I was pedalling away and Tony had again slipped onto a bike beside me, he said after a few seconds---his *first* words---"something wrong?"

It was a direct personal question but I wasn't the least put out---just a little surprised. And there *was* something wrong; our boy, fifteen, had just been caught shop-lifting. No police involved---it was just between us and the shop, a mini market two blocks from our house. Jake had said he was sorry---and off his own bat had offered to do some work for the owner to make amends---but what worried me was *why he had done it.* It can't have been from need---it was just a small block of chocolate. Was it some sort of gesture, and did it portend something worse?

I told Tony all this and he was silent for a while, both of us still pedalling. As we dismounted he said "tell Jake about something disgraceful *you* did when you were his age."

At home later I came to the opinion that he was right; the next morning I angled a conversation to where it seemed natural to tell Jake about the time---the only time---I had cheated in an exam; that evening Jake did open up to me about his 'crime'.

It was a girl; I should have guessed. Inadvertently he told me her name, and I knew her; she is very pretty---but has quite a history. She had challenged Jake---said he'd be 'too scared to do anything'---meaning I suppose anything unlawful. He had stolen the chocolate bar to impress her.

On the Monday when I saw Tony I said "you're brilliant."

 He shook his head and laughed. "I've got teenagers too."

There was a link between us now, and the start I hoped of a friendship.

***

The atmosphere at our tennis nights was changing. More people were now turning up early, and good discussions were starting up, often continuing onto the court itself. And the place was more *cheerful*.

Frank, one of our older men---forthright contributor of one-line declarations--- began to loosen up, so much so that within a few months, if he tackled me on some subject, he would absolutely flood me with words. Where had they been all the time?

Colin, one of our carpenters, had never been backward in expressing an opinion, but in the process he would frequently *mispronounce* words, particularly longer or somewhat unusual ones. At some point during the year that problem disappeared.

Then there was Jane; at the beginning of last year she had looked and acted as she had always done, which was---quiet and unobtrusive.

Most of us turned up in our tennis gear but Jane, because she came straight from work, arrived in her office clothes, and they were, you'd have to say, utilitarian. She never seemed to wear make-up.

On the occasions I had conversed with her I found an intelligent and well informed woman. But her manner was always reserved. She rarely added anything to group discussions---she was just *there*.

One evening though, about the middle of the year---winter anyhow---when I was in the office reception area---a woman who I thought must have been a new member walked in, an attractive, well dressed woman with stylish short blond hair. I looked again---*our Jane*! I let my admiration show---I may have even given a low whistle. I got a smile---and that was the first time I had seen *that*.

With the clothes and the hair seemed to come a new personality. She began to join in our discussions, even telling a joke or two--- some quite ribald. When someone kidded her about having a new boyfriend she said she had *two*. The change was an extreme one--- and, to this observer, extremely interesting.

Finally---Nick. He is one of the youngest members, twenty-five I would guess. He grew up in this town and has a front desk job at the Council offices, dealing with the public. I had been to that office a couple of times and saw how he did the job; he was helpful to people, with a ready smile. A natural.

Nick always *looked* good too---always well groomed. Some of our guys are, shall we say, somewhat casual about such matters, but Nick stands out.

I always thought of him as being boyish for his age. I knew he was not married and I had never seen him with a girl or heard him talk about girls; it had crossed my mind that he might have been gay.

Nick made his big move on that front as we were all talking in the clubhouse after the courts' lights had been turned off. A word of explanation here; although the clubhouse is not licensed we had got into the habit of discreetly bringing in a few drinks on Fridays. I think that was Tony's idea too, and it had been enthusiastically adopted.

At one of these sessions, in about October, Nick was in good form, more than usually talkative; looking back I think that he was preparing himself for the announcement. The opportunity came when the subject of a Christmas party came up; someone jokingly suggested to Jane that she should bring both her boyfriends.

"What about you Nick?" someone else asked, and there was a slight lull in the normal conversational roar; had some of the others thought as I had?

The boy looked around at all of us and there was something in his face I had not seen before---a decidedness.

"Look---I want to tell you all. Some of you have probably guessed anyhow---I'm gay."

There was silence.

Nick continued. "Tonight I'm 'coming out'---to you lot" A smile: a brave one.

I think everyone was stuck for something to say and then laconic Terry, bless him, said "Geez Nick, you blokes always make such a song and dance about it!" Everybody laughed, and conversations ramped up again.

I reached over and gave Nick's shoulder a squeeze; I understood just how big a decision it was that he had just made---it would change his life. Jane walked over and kissed him.

I was moved; it was a real 'moment'. A double moment actually--- my group had proved its cool.

About two months later, at another of our Friday 'soirees', Tony absolutely killed the happy mood by announcing that he would soon be going back to Brisbane. A firm he had once done some work for wanted him to supervise their big new housing development. It could take five years to complete he said, but it could set him up for life.

We all said congratulations and that sort of thing but if the others were feeling as I did it was bad news; he had so enlivened our group.

I bumped into the man the following Sunday morning at our local Farmers Market. He told me his two kids had gone to their mother's in Brisbane for the weekend. My wife had left me alone for the day while she did a district Open Gardens tour with some friends and I asked him back to the house for some lunch. Perfect for a good long talk.

He had been brought up in Adelaide and after high school had travelled for four years, in the Pacific, India and the south of the USA; "I saw Hinduism and Buddhism and a really nice kind of Christianity---- in New Mexico. Tolerant. But I find I have turned away from organised religion. I am prepared to go along with the notion that there is or at least *was* an organising Power---I just can't accept that we have all evolved out of some primeval ooze---but hey, I think we still just don't know enough yet. We're learning so much about the Universe almost day by day aren't we?"

He said that after he returned to Australia he had met an old school mate who was working for a building company in Brisbane; as he needed to earn money quickly he took a job with them as a labourer.

Soon he was training as a carpenter---"I was always good with my hands, and liked making things"---then he went the whole way and became a builder in his own right. "I like designing houses. I probably should have been an architect."

With no time pressures on either of us we ambled through many subjects, eventually lobbing onto 'love and relationships'. He told me his marriage had ended when he and his wife simply came to the realisation that they no longer cared for each other very much.

"And---the old story---Jill had met someone else."

"Unusual for the father to get prime custody of the children."

"I suppose, but that's the way she wanted it---so she could make a clean start with Roger. I was happy---and I've always made sure she has them whenever she wants, and actually that seems to be more and more as time goes on. But that's okay too."

He then told me something arresting---that he was now attracted to *other men*. "Not solely---but definitely."

"Have you ---acted on that?"

"Oh yes."

"That must have been a factor in the break-up with your wife?"

"No. I can honestly say not. I did not become aware of being 'bi' before we split. It sort of snuck up on me afterwards."

I was stuck for words. After a silence he continued. "You know, Kinsey found that very few heterosexual men are 100% that way. We are nearly all somewhere along the scale. If 100% hetero is a 'five' and 100% gay is a 'one' then I think I am a 'four'. Maybe three and a half. How about you?"

I floundered temporarily. "Oh, I'm a 'five' I think."

***

As we walked to his car he told me the move back to Brisbane would be good for his children. "They'll be closer to their mother. This's been a bit hard for her."

"This is going to be hard for *us* too, Tony. We like you very much. I really wish we had had this talk months ago." I was regretting that I hadn't done more in the past months to develop our friendship.

He turned and hugged me---I got a quick kiss on the forehead---and within a few weeks he was back in Brisbane.

***

When it came time to plan our group's Christmas party I offered to have it at our place. I thought Fiona might like to be part of it.

"Have them here by all means but you'll have them on your own. They're *your* friends."

"They're not my *friends*. It's our tennis group. Like your gym group."

"*Not* like my gym group. I can *talk* to them. Some of your mob are throwbacks. That Mullet! And---is it Barry?---does he say *anything*? Can he actually speak?"

"Oh they're not that bad. I told you, they've improved---a lot."

She laughed. "They'd have to. But look, we're having *our* party that night. At the Northern. It's already arranged. I was going to ask *you*."

***

So I hosted the party on my own; everyone brought their own meat and grog and I made up some salads. There seemed to be a mountain of food but it disappeared in a very short time.

Around eleven when I was in the kitchen scratching the ingredients together for a big omelette I was joined by young Nick. I asked him to break eggs into a bowl.

"Keep me company. Watch the master at work. I've got a great cheese to go in this. Tony told me about it."

He said it was our great loss that Tony had decided to go back to the big smoke.

"Yes. I don't mind admitting to you Nick I was quite downcast when he told me he was going. Someone once said that your true family is scattered across the world and if you're lucky you find some of them. He could have been my brother."

"I loved him too---but not as a brother."

"You didn't seduce our unsuspecting friend did you Nick?"

He laughed and leaned back against the counter. "Did you already know I was gay?"

"I thought you might have been."

"I think Tony worked it out fairly quickly. Our conversations at the tennis were always 'straight' but I was attracted to him. Who wouldn't be? Then one day he suggested we go for a drink at the Sportsman's and, well, it turned out the attraction was mutual."

"When did this happen?"

"Oh---sometime in winter."

He said that it was Tony who had helped him make up his mind to reveal his sexuality. "He made it sound so---inevitable---he took away my fears. Country town attitudes---you know......"

"How has that been?"

"Not too bad actually. I've got some good friends. *This* mob has been fantastic." That too was partly Tony's doing I thought; he'd opened up a few minds there.

Later, when I was with Colin, I asked him how he had overcome the mispronunciation thing.

"Tony! Well, Tony's advice. He put me onto this phonics teacher."

"It didn't seem to take long."

"Six weeks! We got Barry there too."

And then---Jane. She and I were in a quiet corner of the garden talking about our plans for the year ahead. She said she would be staying in town and intended to keep coming to the tennis: "But it isn't as good without Tony."

"No, he was a real asset."

"I will be eternally grateful to him."

She said it with such feeling that I looked hard at her; she did not meet my eyes but even though there was not much light where we were sitting I could tell she was beginning to blush.

"Jane, what…..?"

She shook her head but she was smiling too. "*You're* the psychologist….."

"Did you and he…..?"

She nodded.

She said she had been sexually inexperienced when she married and never had an orgasm with her husband. By the time of their divorce she had come to believe she was destined not to enjoy sex. "Just one of those women, you know. There seem to be quite a lot of us. I've had opportunities since then of course but I never felt confident enough to take them."

Somehow---and I could imagine it---she had found herself telling Tony all this *and he had offered to help.*

"We went to bed together several times at my flat. It was perfect---*he* was perfect---I think he could make a living at it! He was so relaxed, and it made me the same."

This must have happened I thought at much the same time as the Nick thing. I didn't of course mention that but, with it on my mind, I said this was amazing and she said yes wasn't it and laughed and it was the *best* laugh. What I would call unbridled.

***

When I was in the kitchen again, making the late stayers some toasted sandwiches, a thought stopped me in my tracks. *Had I too changed over the year?*

 Hard to say about oneself, but I thought maybe I had---a bit. My two kids seemed to be responding to me more, and to be more affectionate. And I had overheard one of my daughter's girlfriends say she thought I was 'cool'. Praise indeed from a teenager.

So---maybe.

***

I went to bed about two; I didn't hear Fiona come in but she had said she would probably sleep in the guest bedroom. In the morning I was in the kitchen attending to the huge mess when she surfaced.

"Good night?" I asked.

"Terrific. How was yours? Lots of 'incorrect' jokes?"

"Of course. And very funny."

"Mmmmm."

"Jake thought so." To stir.

"What! You didn't let him come out?"

"He got up about ten and said he couldn't sleep. The noise."

"And you let him stay up?"

155

"Actually he spent most of his time with Barry."

"Good God! If he …."

"Relax. They played pool for about half an hour and then I sent him back to bed." Actually an hour and a half; what had stayed my hand was seeing the big quiet man patiently showing my son how to improve his game. I had watched them occasionally from the next room. It is perhaps an odd adjective to use but I had found it charming.

"Well---somehow I don't think I missed anything interesting."

"That's a bit elitist dear" I said, but I was thinking that *I* had heard quite a bit that was interesting, and that I dare say *she* would have found interesting too.

***

After I had cleaned up the place that morning to my perfectionist wife's satisfaction and was taking a breather, the last 'interesting' event of the evening came back to me; *the ever silent Barry had spoken.*

He had been the very last to leave. We had played one final game of pool and I walked with him to his car. As he unlocked it he turned towards me.

"It's a pity about Tony going" he said. "New people are good."

FIFTEEN

JUST GIRLS

It had taken her a long time to get to her seat in the school hall, in the section that had been reserved for parents. She was surprised that so many people had turned up, and also that she *knew* so many of them; not being a Catholic herself Janet had expected she would know very few. Most of those she *did* know were not Catholics either, and she wondered if they had chosen the nuns' school for the same reason she and Ted had---because they believed that there was more care and discipline here than at the State.

Seated, she looked around, still receiving waves and smiles. *Nervous* smiles she thought, if they are like me---wondering if our darlings will get through their pieces without disaster.

It had been nice that both girls had decided to learn instruments; lately it seemed there was always the sound of a violin or a clarinet coming from some part of the homestead. While she did have a general impression that they were progressing---slowly---she had been astonished when they told her they were going to play in the annual concert. It was a pity that the rain had forced Ted to stay home tonight to finish the sorghum sowing.

She had been greeted at the door by Nadine and Claire, the very first friends she had made when she moved to the town from the southern coast years before. Their own children were grown even then, and now their grandchildren had also left the school, but the two had remained staunch 'Friends' of St. Thérèse's.

"We've made ourselves the official welcomers," Claire said, as they fussed over her two girls.

Settled now into the happy buzz of noise around her, she thought---this will be a lovely night. Being met by Nadine and Claire had made it even nicer; she wondered if they too were reminded of their first meetings. I was just a girl then, she thought.

***

She had started to question if the afternoon walk had been a good idea. It was still so hot---it must have been thirty-five degrees---and although the morning had been clear with a light breeze there was now a thin high covering of cloud and the breeze had disappeared. The sun burned through the cloud, and the humidity had increased. In her four weeks in the town Janet had already learned that this could mean rain in a day or two's time but, before that, uncomfortable sticky heat. It wasn't sticky yet but she thought it could be by evening.

The bigger question though was---had she made a mistake in accepting the teaching position here? It wasn't just the heat and humidity that was making her think this, it was Waltham itself: so far north---so far inland---so *small.*

The teaching itself was good---she was happy with that---and the children were well mannered, but after a month she still felt out of place. She was finding it hard to *talk* with people---with the parents. They seemed so wrapped up in their own activities, and with the particulars of country life---which were physical ones, like the weather and crops and livestock. She wasn't part of that life---she was not fitting in. She had not met anyone so far with whom she could share her own interests of literature and music.

Before and after school she was kept busy preparing lessons, and that was good, but she longed to have a real conversation with someone---and not about school or cattle or the weather---and it hadn't happened. She found she was scarcely meeting anyone outside of school hours.

Weekends were the worst---they seemed interminable. And how long would it stay this *hot*? She would have to find her own place to rent, one with an air-conditioner. But for now, on this Sunday, she was trying to walk off the afternoon heat in the back streets of her new town---a flat and, she had to say, fairly unattractive town---unattractive compared to the coastal towns she knew, with their green hills and their views.

She decided to walk in the direction of the convent. At least there were some shady peppercorn trees along the front of it---and there might be a nun in the garden there to talk to.

***

She was still a block and a half from the old double-storeyed building when she heard the violin. She did not recognise the tune before the playing stopped. She kept walking and the playing began again, but stopped once more after a few seconds.

She crossed the road to the stone wall that fronted the convent. As she neared the centre gate with its wrought iron archway the playing started again. It was louder now, and she realised it was coming from the building itself. It was a different piece, and she recognised a long solo from the Brahms Concerto. She stopped in the shade of a peppercorn and leaned against the wall.

The violinist played with skill and confidence; it struck her as incongruous that such assured playing should be coming from such a place. And where exactly *was* it coming from? All the French doors along the top and bottom floors were closed---as was the big central front door---and there seemed to be nobody on the verandahs.

There were screens of lattice here and there along all the verandahs and now she noticed movement behind one section upstairs, near the corner of the building; the violinist was there.

The playing continued and, it seemed to Janet, with growing power. In volume and intensity it dominated that hushed afternoon, the liquid sound sweeping out across the lawn and over her and the peppercorns. She imagined it must have been covering all of Waltham, house by house and street by street. Did it cross the river and roll out across the grasslands beyond? Could any amount of distance stop it? It was mesmerising.

She was shocked from her reverie by someone's voice.

"It's lovely isn't it?" A woman of perhaps forty-five was standing beside her. "She started last Sunday. I live just there," pointing across the road. Claire Foster introduced herself, and together they listened until the playing stopped and they saw the French door behind the lattice open and close.

***

The following Sunday Janet walked to the convent half an hour earlier. Again the violin was played; she was listening in the same spot when Claire appeared, but this time with two little folding chairs.

The concert lasted nearly an hour and at the end Claire invited her back for afternoon tea. She met Claire's husband Reg, a mechanic, who worked on a farm not far out of town. Claire had learned piano as a girl; she played some Rodgers and Hammerstein, and the two women sang.

The next Sunday Claire turned up with an extra chair and after a few minutes her friend Nadine appeared. The woman seemed to know a lot about music---sometimes she would 'conduct'.

There were tears in Nadine's eyes at the conclusion of a slow Bartok piece; "oh, that was lovely. She can play." At the end Janet clapped the performer. The other two joined in---but there was no acknowledgement from the lattice.

The three of them went back to Claire's again and lingered over an afternoon tea until six o'clock. Nadine had a strong soprano; she sang "Songs My Mother Taught Me" and "The Last Rose of Summer."

The women told Janet their stories; they were both locals, daughters of station workers. They had both done well at school but their parents had not wanted them to go away to college or university. They had both married at the age of twenty-one.

***

The Sunday afternoon concert and the time with Claire and Nadine afterwards became for her the highlight of the week---and she found she was beginning to accept her new home. Within a month of the first recital she realised she had ceased to feel homesick. But she didn't ever meet or even see the soloist, and while the other two were accepting of this she longed to change that.

When the concert finished the women always applauded for a few seconds, not loud but enough to carry across the lawn. At the end of perhaps the eighth recital Janet clapped louder, but as usual the French doors closed with no acknowledgement. The other women began folding their chairs but something impelled her to keep clapping. She stared at the closed door. Acknowledge. Accept our thanks. Please. She kept clapping and after a few seconds the door opened, a hand appeared around the end of the lattice and gave a little wave and then the door closed again.

And that was to be the end of it. The following Sunday there was no playing; after waiting for an hour the women adjourned to Claire's. It was the same the following Sunday. Nadine said she'd find out what she could and a few days later rang Janet to say that all she had learned was that no nun had left the convent and no nun was ill.

Claire told her a month later that she had never heard the violin again. The little wave of acknowledgement had also been one of goodbye.

***

The night's big orchestral piece went off without a hitch and, as far as she could tell, with no false starts or wrong notes from any of the children. Sister Barbara, according to her girls, was a very good teacher, and she thought that the woman had chosen the Strauss piece well, with its definite beat and strong melodies.

When the nun turned to acknowledge the applause Janet saw a confident handsome woman. She was wearing a blue well-fitted dress; no makeup but a silver necklace and a silver brooch.

After the children had traipsed from the stage the woman picked up a violin and sat herself on a stool near the front of the stage. At the first few notes Janet straightened in her seat; she had not heard Maessen's "Air" since those Sunday afternoon recitals.

Now as the playing continued she felt sure she was listening to that same person. There was the accomplished phrasing, the same boldness. When it was finished, the woman gave a real performer's bow to acknowledge the applause.

***

At the end of the concert she made her way to the stage and introduced herself. "You have lovely girls," the nun said. Close up, Janet realised that the woman was no older than herself.

"We have met before in a way. I used to come and listen at the wall under the peppercorns on a Sunday afternoon."

The nun stopped collecting the music sheets. "You were the one who clapped."

"Yes. I loved it. I'd just come here, you see, and I was homesick. You---changed that."

"I'm glad."

"Why did you stop though?"

A wry smile. "Mother. She disapproved I'm afraid."

"But you're playing now…..?"

"Yes---well---times have changed."

The nun began folding the music stands and Janet helped her, stacking them to one side of the stage.

"My girls talk a lot about you. They love all this."

"We'll meet again then."

"Yes. And not in twelve years time."

As Janet walked to the steps that led down to the auditorium she heard the nun say something. She turned.

"I'm sorry?"

"It's alright. I was thinking aloud. I said---I was just a girl."

SIXTEEN

SHOW TIME

'Community involvement' takes on real meaning when you are on a Show Committee.

Last night our President called us all to the Poultry and Caged Birds Pavilion. Earlier Sam Perrett had gone there to check the power points and to bed down some of his budgerigars. He found the rafters swarming with rats.

Ordinarily we would have put down rat poison, but we were now only two days out from the Show; the public could not be asked to pick their way around the smelly carcases of hundreds of rats. Other quicker and more physical means were called for.

The whole committee plus friends gathered as many rat traps as we could and converged. Several people brought their dogs as well, the idea being that they would catch on the floor what the traps up in the rafters did not.

The traps worked well but the dogs were a mistake. There were just too many energetic, aggressive dogs in the one place and they began to get stuck into each other instead of the rats. It was chaos---the din in that corrugated iron building was horrific.

We called a halt, something which itself took nearly half an hour, and decided to take the dogs home. "We need some cats," said someone, a suggestion that met with general approval though I, for one, was doubtful.

The cat initiative was successful---initially---but our cats do like to climb, and soon some were themselves being caught in the traps.

I do not know if you have ever seen a cat who has just set off a rat trap with its tail. It screeches and leaps into the air---in this case to land on the floor of the shed---and then it takes off like a rocket. We had wisely shut the doors so any such cat careened around and around. When there were three or four doing this at the same time it was best to get out of the way, though some owners, unwisely I thought, tried to catch their pets with their bare hands. There was a lot of cursing and shouting and, disgraceful to admit, a lot of laughing from those not directly involved.

Actually, I don't recall when I last laughed so much at the show ground; it could have been the time when our previous Ringmaster tried to divert the attentions of the champion Shorthorn bull from a nubile heifer during the Grand Parade; the lesson we all learned that day was never to get between two such animals, or, if one does, to stay on one's feet. But I digress.

Eventually all the cats were caught, by using horse rugs to throw over them. They were taken home as large bundles and I don't know how people got the traps off them, but I will bet quite a few of our citizens are sporting scratches today. Back in the shed we decided to rely on the traps and just one dog, Sam Perrett's old Corgi. It was a lot quieter.

By eleven o'clock it was very cold and someone got a fire going in a big drum. We threw the dead rats into the fire. Some of the more thoughtful ones had brought along rum and we found some pannikins. After a while we did not notice the cold and I am afraid even tended to forget about the rats. Even the Corgi gave up.

Occasionally a trap *would* go off and one of us would wander off to investigate.

***

We did not kill *all* the rats. When I went up again today I saw one in the roof, and Sam tells me he has seen several. But---good enough; once again the Show Committee has saved the day.

I can recall one occasion when we did fall short. We had not been able to locate enough straw bedding for the horse stalls and we decided to bring in fresh shavings from the sawmill. It stained all the horses that lay in it: strong stain too, that could not be washed off. The committee had to explain to an incredulous judge why the hacks at our show had such bright and unusual markings. The horse exhibitors were outraged and kicked up a big fuss---but the horse people are always difficult.

SEVENTEEN

MAGGIE

I like bantams, especially bantam hens. There is something about the look of them that is very appealing to me---the curves of neck and tail, the way the feathers so perfectly overlay each other---those bright eyes, that quick appreciation of any situation---and their busy ways. They are efficient little managers of their lives, and of course brilliant rearers of chicks.

I keep quite a number of real laying hens, Rhode Island Reds and big black Australorps, but I always have a few bantams as well, to hatch settings of eggs and, really, just because I like them so much. They are much friendlier than my other hens; if any of my chooks gather around me when I am sitting on my back steps it is invariably these little ladies. I put grain on my boots and they peck it off; some even jump onto my knee and take it from my hand, even allowing me to stroke them.

One orange ball of fluff has a brood of six chicks at present; strictly speaking they are an Australorp's, but though they are quite the wrong colour, and already half the size of their foster mother---at just two weeks---this little one believes they are all her own work, and is fiercely protective of them.

This hen was the favourite of my old friend Maggie. When she called in on one of her walks through town she would sit with me on these steps, or on the bench under the peppercorn, and Orange would always jump up on her lap, and stay there as long as the visit lasted.

Maggie asked me not long ago if the hen had ever reared chickens and when I said no she begged me to allow it. "Just because she's little doesn't mean she couldn't be a good mother." When the hen did go broody just a few weeks ago I gave her a setting; she hatched them all, and *is* rearing them very well---but sadly my friend will never see them.

***

I remember first sighting Maggie Fitch in the main street of our town shortly after I moved into the district in the early 1960's; she was the smallest woman I had ever seen, just 130 centimetres--- perhaps even less. She was wearing jodhpurs and a long sleeved shirt, which I would learn was her favourite attire. Her hair, black and very long, hung down her back in one thick plait.

Locals told me she rode racehorses for her father, exercising and helping to train them. She also did casual work for people, secretarial and gardening. She never drove but walked everywhere, and briskly. She had a somewhat severe expression but I learned it broke into a nice smile when she said hello. Bright eyes. She would I suppose have then been about thirty.

While I was living for the next twenty years or so out on our cattle property I would see her only occasionally, at a race meeting or when I came to town, but when I settled here after my wife died I would see her quite often: still moving quickly, a little dynamo.

She had kept her hair long, but now coiled on top of her head, and held in place with one of those large Spanish combs. She also now wore skirts, unusual ones that probably were specially made; they were tight at the waist, long, and very full at the hem, often of a heavy material, and when she walked, with her long brisk stride, they swung. She wore Cubans, those elastic sided riding boots that have a high heel; she still wore long-sleeved shirts, not blouses. The effect was Argentinian---imagine a small female gaucho.

***

Perhaps a year after I had relocated myself here, and with my growing business interests taking a lot of my time, I advertised in our local paper for someone to clean my house and do the washing and ironing, and the first person to answer the ad was Maggie.

Early one morning, while I was sitting on the steps leading off my side verandah reading the previous day's "Australian", she walked in off the street and said "I'll do it"---just like that.

I was surprised. For one thing there was her age; I had envisaged a younger woman, a stay-at-home mother perhaps; Maggie then would have been in her fifties. Also, I thought the modest amount I was offering would not have been attractive to her ---it was generally known that she had been left comfortably off by her family---but when I raised the subject of pay, a little embarrassedly, she brushed it aside. "Doesn't matter. You need help and I've got the time."

The *big* question in my mind though concerned her stature; would she actually be able to handle the work? Could she *reach* any of the clothes that were at the bottom of my washing machine, or stand up above my ironing board? As for washing the taller windows.......?

She came once or sometimes twice a week, worked the whole morning---and managed everything perfectly. She found herself a sturdy wooden box to stand on in the laundry and at the ironing board, and she used my folding steps for dusting high shelves and mantelpieces. The top sections of my sash windows *were* beyond her but I had forbidden that anyhow because I was worried she might fall; we did those windows as a team.

Employer and employee quickly became friends, and she shared her history with me. Her parents had not married until they were in their late thirties, by which time Reg, who had been a stockman then overseer on one of our bigger district cattle properties, had drawn a block in a land ballot just to the east of the town. He worked hard on the place, Maggie told me, but had just got it into reasonable order when a worsening hip problem made it difficult for him to continue, and they decided to sell.

Though the property was small by district standards it fetched a high price, largely because of its proximity to town (but I know it well, and it is also very good country). The trio was able to live off interest on the invested proceeds, in a house in town.

Reg Fitch was a keen horseman, and had trained a few racehorses for local people as a hobby, and after he moved to town he decided to do more of this. He employed a succession of strappers and jockeys, with Maggie also riding and exercising the horses.

"I remember Maggie at those race meetings," a local friend Mary Carmody told me. "She handled those horses like they were farmyard pets. She didn't ride them in the actual races though; I don't think female jockeys were allowed then."

"Was she always small? At school?"

"No, not as a young girl---primary school. Average I would have said. Oh, a little below; Reg and Mildred were both short. No---it seemed to be from about twelve or so she just stopped growing. She filled out in the other ways, but she stayed tiny .What is she---four feet?"

"I'd say. And never married?"

"No. No boyfriend either, that I can remember. I suppose being so tiny ......

Pity though, she would have made someone a very good wife."

Once when Maggie told me that someone we both knew was a good mother and I said that *she* would have made a good one, she joked that she wouldn't have had room to carry a baby for nine months.

"Do you know why you didn't grow any taller?"

"No. And none of the doctors did either. A mystery." She said it in a matter of fact tone---in no way sad or bitter---but I suppose there would have been times.........

***

I learned a lot about the history of our town from Maggie, as she passed on stories she had heard from the old timers. We'd talk about world affairs too; she was well informed, and certainly had opinions. They were delivered with firmness---perhaps a little dogmatically---but she did listen to my attempts to put alternative ones. I gained the impression that she did not often exchange serious views or have discussions with many other people.

***

She stopped working for me about five years ago, when she was approaching seventy. I had been trying to persuade her to stop for years before but I think she may just have enjoyed the contact. She still dropped in once a week though.

But now, unexpectedly, my friend is no more. Taking to her bed with a bad cold, she had contracted pneumonia. She lived alone, and none of us had thought to check on her until it was too late. I share the blame for that.

***

I have one more thing I need to do for her now; I am her executor. Her wishes were simple; as she had no living relatives I am to sell her house and give the proceeds and the rest of her funds to the local schools. I can dispose of her personal effects as I see fit.

I decided to ask our mutual friend Mary to come with me to Maggie's house while I catalogued her possessions. I thought that if there were saleable items there she might have a better idea of their values and how we might realise on them. Also, frankly, I was uncomfortable at the thought of going through Maggie's home and possessions on my own; I wanted another person with me, preferably a woman, and Mary was ideal.

We soon saw that the crockery and cutlery was just of an every-day quality and in addition there seemed to be no special collectables or display items. The furniture was 1920's and fairly plain; I thought that we might as well give everything to our local 'Vinnies'.

***

Mary began going through the clothing in the wardrobe of what was obviously Maggie's bedroom. She said that everything was so tiny they would not fit anybody else. I went out into the kitchen to start boxing up some of the crockery.

A few minutes later she called to me, some excitement in her voice; I found her in the second bedroom. She was standing before the open doors of a built- in wardrobe that extended right along one wall, and was holding a garment across each arm.

"These are gorgeous Hugh. Look at the beading on this." She held up a long black dress that glittered even under the dim light of the small overhead bulb. "And the embroidery on this!"

She laid the garments on the bed and brought out two more. "Oh, beautiful."

"I can smell camphor."

"Yes, she looked after them. I can't see any moth damage, or even any wear. They're immaculate. And they are full size. Maggie never wore any of these."

"They look pretty old."

"1930's and 40's. Oh, you don't get material like this now." She held up another dress to the light. "Hugh, they're beautifully made."

"This is a mystery then. Who did they belong to?"

Mary stood still for a moment, then turned to me. "I don't know, but I think her mother could have made these. She was a dressmaker and had a very good reputation. My own mother had things made by her. But dressmakers don't usually do beading and embroidery."

"Could Maggie have done that?"

"Yes. She was very good at craftwork. Very clever with those little hands."

"But if they were made for clients---how would Maggie end up with them?"

"Well---I don't know---perhaps she just asked people if she could have them after they had worn them a few times ...."

"But they are immaculate you said. Hardly worn at all."

"Hugh, the women who had these made for them would have had money. Like my mother. Like me. We don't wear good outfits over and over, or even special ones. *Particularly* special ones. No, she wouldn't have had a problem getting these back."

"So---why?"

"I suppose we will never know for sure."

"Well---in memory of her mother? Keepsakes. And she *had* done some of the work..."

"Or---Hugh---dreaming of what might have been? If she had grown to normal height, been a 'normal' person, she would have worn things like these." She took another garment from the rack. "This is a ball gown. Shantung." She held it up against herself. "You could wear this today. But little Maggie didn't go to balls. She never did. She must have thought no-one would dance with her. Sad...."

We were silent a moment then I shook myself up. "If these are so good maybe we can sell them?"

Mary turned towards me. "Do you have complete say about what to do with them?"

"Yes. Why?"

"I think we should keep them."

"*Keep* them?"

"In our museum. A new section---'Social History'. That place is too masculine anyhow. All those implements and tools!"

"Well---I am on the Museum Committee. We *could*....." I looked up at the ceiling. "Would that be okay Maggie?"

"Of course it would. And if that penny-pinching committee of your's won't buy some decent cabinets I will pay for them myself. These have to be properly displayed. And *I'll* do the information cards. I know someone who's fantastic on old fashions. And I think it won't be too hard to find out who used to own these.

This will be very interesting."

Mary went on pulling dresses out; I was leaning against a tall chest and for something to do I pulled open the top drawer. In it were two packages side by side, wrapped in tissue paper. I took out one, laid it on the bed and unwrapped what looked to be a shirt---very small---yellow, with a diagonal brown stripe.

"Oh," Mary said, "a jockey's silk."

"It's tiny."

"It was hers, look" and she pointed to 'Maggie' embroidered on the left shoulder. I took out the second package out and unwrapped it.

"Another one. Identical."

"Not quite" Mary said. She pointed to the name 'Tom.'

"Who would that have been?"

"Tom---Tom---" Mary repeated to herself. "There *was* a Tom. One of the young jockeys Reg employed. Tom---oh, what was his name? I remember he came from the coast. He eventually went back to the family farm there---a dairy. Yes, he used to ride at the meetings. He was good looking too, a nice open face. He was very popular. And Maggie would have spent a lot of time with him."

She picked up one of the silks and took it to the light. "They're nicely done. Her mother would have made these too. And Maggie might have done the names." She turned towards me. "Hugh, do you think they….?" She raised her eyebrows.

" What?" but I knew; I'd seen Mary before when she thought she had discovered a love secret of one of her friends.

"Well---side by side in the drawer---that's a clue. And why not? They were together a lot---they were young......."

"She never mentioned him to me."

"Why would she? So long ago…"

"Well, we did talk about life. And love. A bit."

"Oh Hugh, let's keep these too." She replaced the silk on the bed beside the other and moved the sleeves so that that they were touching. She smiled. "Holding hands."

***

When I saw Mary a few days later she told me she had taken all the clothes to her own dressmaker---"just to fix any little thing"---and that she had already tracked down the owners of some of the dresses. I promised to talk to the Museum Committee.

"We'll need a lot of display cases." she warned. "And I'm going to need a special little one for the two silks."

***

Now as I sit under my Jacaranda I am thinking about my little departed friend. I miss her.

Orange is beside me with her chicks---the chicks that she thinks are entirely hers. I have decided to rename her Maggie. And acquire a bantam rooster---and call him Tom.

EIGHTEEN

A GOOD DAY'S WORK

I am not driving particularly fast this morning but I keep hitting birds. I try slowing down but this has no effect---even when I drop right back to forty. Blowing the horn doesn't work either---the birds seem determined to ignore me. Three times I have gone right through flocks of galahs that have stayed on the road until it was too late.

I've noticed this phenomenon on other occasions but mostly just before sunset. I remember one afternoon I hit virtually every crested pigeon that was on the road. I didn't want to of course---hated it---but those birds, that are usually so adept at avoiding cars, had sat that day as if mesmerised. It was at sorghum harvest time and I put it down to the fact that they had been gorging on the grain that had spilled from trucks, and perhaps they had been just too heavy to make a quick getaway. Except that didn't explain why they had *delayed* their attempts to escape; it was almost as if they were drugged. *Could* they have been, I have wondered---by something in the grain?

I see quite a few magpies this morning, but they are different. Of all the birds I think the black and white ones look after themselves best. You never hit a magpie.

***

My daughter-in-law had phoned the previous night to say that the buyers were due to call at our property to look at cattle but Ralph had hurt his back and wouldn't be able to do the muster. They would have to cancel unless I could come out from town.

"It's just a pulled muscle Dad. They were moving one of those heavy pipes in the yards and he tripped over a fig root and instead of just letting his end go he tried to hold it up. Stupid man. He just needs to rest it for a couple of days but he's too sore now. He can't even turn over without whimpering." She had chuckled; Ralph, my energetic, quicksilver second son, wouldn't be a patient patient.

***

I reach the property by eight-thirty but the buyers are not due till eleven so I can spend some time with Ralph and Sally and the kids. Ralph is now walking, but very stiffly, and he grimaces when he turns. Sally makes us a coffee; by contrast she is brisk and cheerful.

"We told them they were a very even lot and they said in that case we wouldn't need to put them in the yards. Holding them in a corner of a paddock would do. They're in 'Little Creek'." Ralph catches my eye and we both grin. "What?"

"It's their first ploy Sally," I tell her. "If I don't like their offer---and I'm sure I won't---they will then tell me there is actually quite a lot of variation in the cattle and we'll have to take them to the yards and draft them up."

"And that even if they do come up a bit on the best ones they'll have to come back on the others," Ralph adds, "and the price will probably work out the same, overall."

"Yep. By the way, do we know these hombres?"

"No---first time here."

"Good. Do we have any weights?"

"I weighed a bunch of them last week." Ralph hands me a list of figures.

"Wise move."

"And I put the scales out of sight in the shed."

"Even wiser. Who taught you these tricks?"

***

Sally lends me her own horse and by a quarter to eleven Rocky and I have the mob nicely settled in a corner of 'Little Creek', with the help of Craig the young ringer. I am ready in more than one way; I know the current auction rates, and Ralph, Sally and I have agreed on our prices. I also know we still have plenty of sorghum crop left, if we decide to hold them over.

The men arrive, we introduce ourselves, and even as we shake hands they are casting their eyes over the cattle. We have bought the best Santa Gertrudis and Droughtmaster bulls we could afford over the last twenty years, and these steers show the benefit. John and Brendan give no sign of it but I am confident they are impressed; I doubt if they will have seen a better mob of well finished, well bred cattle. They display the usual mien of professional cattle buyers however, friendly but non-committal, in no way seeming keen to buy.

Their first offer comes and I frown. "I'm sure they're worth more than that. We've been looking at the auctions in Rockhampton. They seem to be very strong." Then I add, as if the thought has just struck me, "they're near your works. If we trucked them in you could bid on them there."

This idea has absolutely no appeal. Once word got around that three hundred heavy prime were coming in from the 'Run' every big meat buyer in central Queensland would be interested. There would be no chance of these men setting their own prices then.

There is actually, they inform me now, some variation amongst them. "We probably should take them to the yards and draft them up. We might be able to come up a bit on the best of them but we'd have to come back on some of the others," John says, soberly.

"Yes," says Brendan, "and actually it'll probably average out at much the same," he says to me, and to John he adds, as if in afterthought, "we have to be at the Flemings by two, don't we?"

"We'd better get a move on then" I say, and urge Rocky forward; I have heard it all before. Craig and I push the cattle along the fence towards the yards. Within half an hour we have them in and our visitors are working the drafting gates. I borrow their Nissan and go back to the house for a thermos of tea.

'How's it going?" Sally asks.

"Oh, the usual. They're drafting them now. They're six cents a kilogram under but I think they'll come up." Six cents would mean more than thirty dollars a head.

"Or we won't sell?"

"Or we won't sell. Next time it's your turn to do this."

"Oh no, I couldn't do it. It's a man's game. It seems silly to me, you all *know* the values and you all know what the results will be."

"Ah, but sometimes these guys realise we *don't* know the values. And sometimes, even when we do, we give in."

"*You* don't. I should go down and warn those men."

"Too late. We're best friends already. But I might take a few sandwiches with me. This could take a while."

When I arrive back John is on his satellite phone, reporting on the situation to his boss I assume. The drafting has been completed and the men have done a good job. Each of the three groups is certainly more even now---but this has really been only an exercise; at the regular fat sale in Rockhampton these steers, in my opinion, would sell pen after pen---undrafted---at the one price, and probably for more than the figure the men first offered. In fact, a line as big and as good as ours generally creates a buzz that can push prices *up* as an auction proceeds.

"You've done a nice job" I say. Sixty percent of the cattle have made it into their 'top' line. "But you can't expect to have the tops for that sort of money." I ask for ten cents above their first offer for these and, a little to my surprise, they agree quite quickly. They have decided on this while I was away.

"We'll take these too," John says, indicating the next largest group, "but they're a bit light. We don't like handling anything under five hundred kilograms."

They don't believe we have scales, I think. Good on you Ralph. "They'd be *over* five" I say.

"No way," and they look at each other and shake their heads--- sadly---as if this were a matter of personal sorrow to them. They're good.

"Why don't we weigh some Mr. Watson?" innocent young Craig suggests.

" Good idea."

The men do not show any reaction to the news that we have scales, and in fact help us lift them out of the shed and place them on the floor of the crush. The first beast of this line registers five hundred and sixty kilograms and the next half dozen average five hundred and forty. The men call a halt at that. They still want to drop five cents off the top price but I dig in at two and, again quite quickly, they agree. I am on a roll.

"We definitely can't take these though," they tell me, indicating the third group. "They're not finished. We'd have to feed them for at least six weeks."

I doubt this; take away the tops and the remainder would still sell at Rockhampton as prime. I count them and there are fifty-six, *exactly* the number that would fill a double decker. They do want them--- but they want a bargain.

"We have plenty of sorghum left. We can put them back," I say, and move as if to let them out into the holding yard.

"We *could* take them, but we'd have to come back a fair bit." We begin the real haggle now; they offer ten cents less than the previous price---I say two---they move to eight. I concede to three---and there we stop.

We pour cups of tea and open up the sandwiches and talk of other things: the State of Origin, the Dry. Brendan tells me he used to ride with my other son Bill at Pony Club.

***

When we get back to business we settle on a five cent drop. They use their phone to book trucks for the next day, ask to be told when we have another mob for sale, and are on their way by one-thirty.

***

In the evening, I sit in the homestead's big kitchen while Sally cooks and Ralph, a bit more comfortable, lets the boys climb all over him on the old lounge that we have brought in for him from another room. It's a scene that this father and grandfather relishes.

"We'll feed these two and get them off to bed before we eat," Sally says.

"That Rocky of yours is terrific," I tell her. "You've done a good job on him." Sally is a good horsewoman.

"It's mostly him. He's a natural."

Ralph has been fiddling with a small calculator. "You did well Dad. You got an extra sixteen thousand dollars out of those robbers. Not a bad day's work."

***

Early the next morning I hear on the ABC that Japan has announced two large new beef tenders. Prices are expected to jump immediately---and John and Brendan would have known this.

I help Craig and the truckies load the cattle, have an early lunch and begin to drive back to town. I listen to the Country Hour and learn that during the morning's sale at Rockhampton prices have increased *twenty cents*.

***

I come round a bend and see two magpies standing in the road. They see me but I know I do not need to slow down; you never hit a magpie.

THE WRITER

 Ron Iddon is probably best known in Australia for his work on the ABC's long running television series "A BIG COUNTRY", as reporter and director.

He left the ABC to become an independent filmmaker, eventually writing and directing twenty more documentaries, all of which were shown on television; "Peppimenarti", about life in an Aboriginal settlement in the Northern Territory, was nominated for 'Best Documentary' in the AFI Awards.

He has three published co-written non-fiction books to his credit, and in late 2011 produced a volume of fiction ("The Short Stories of Ron Iddon---The Murray River Collection", released by the publisher of this book, Leopardwood Productions).

Ron lives in Toowoomba, southern Queensland. He writes every day, and is also a part-time teacher in literacy; his recreation is the study and restoration of antique furniture.

EARLIER BOOKS BY THIS AUTHOR

NON-FICTION

(In collaboration)

A Big Country (John Mabey)

A Big Country, 2 (John Mabey)

The Stockman (Mary Durack, R.M. Williams et al)

FICTION

(Solo)

The Short Stories of Ron Iddon---The Murray River Collection

Both 'The Murray River Collection' and 'The Queensland
Collection' are available only on the internet.

 **LEOPARDWOOD PRODUCTIONS**

www.leopardwoodproductions.com.au